more advance]

PROOF OI

"*Proof of Me* is such a beautifully textured book. Every sentence of Lazure's prose is stamped with authority and confidence, allowing the people, place, situations, and descriptions a rich and satisfying dimensionality."

— AIMEE BENDER

author of *The Butterfly Lampshade*

"Erica Plouffe Lazure's *Proof of Me* is a striking debut collection. Put your ear to the page and you will hear trace vibrations of O'Connor, Welty, Hannah and others, but the prose is all her own. Lazure's sentences are richly textured, sensory, and alive with dark comedy and pitiless observation. As for the characters, she has clearly been watching them all her life."

— SVEN BIRKERTS

author of *Changing the Subject: Art and Attention in the Internet Age*

"If you can imagine Flannery O'Connor watching *Wheel of Fortune* or hearing a bad version of 'Bohemian Rhapsody' at karaoke night, that might give you some idea of Erica Plouffe Lazure's *Proof of Me*. In these darkly comic linked stories, the reader encounters a meticulous eye for detail, a keen ear for American voices, and an astringent sympathy for men who mow their lawns 'bare-chested, pot-belly proud' and women who know 'there's always problems with the mens, long as there been mens.'"

— DAVID GATES

author of *A Hand Reached Down to Guide Me*

Sugar Mountain: Stories

Heard Around Town

Dry Dock

PROOF OF ME
AND OTHER STORIES

ERICA PLOUFFE LAZURE

newamericanpress

Milwaukee, Wisconsin

newamericanpress

© 2022 by Erica Plouffe Lazure

Printed in the United States of America

ISBN 9781941561270

Book design by Brian Matzat and Angelo Maneage
Story illustrations by Erica Plouffe Lazure
Cover design by Brian Matzat

The stories in this collection were first published in the following journals: "Cadence" in *McSweeney's Quarterly Concern*; "Selvage" in the *Greensboro Review*; "Distance" in *Booth*; "The Ghost Rider" in *Carve Magazine*; "Stacks" in *Fiction Southeast*; "The Shit Branch" in *Tahoma Journal*; "Marchers" in *American Short Fiction*; "The Cold Front" in *The New Guard*; "Gestate" in the *Raleigh News & Observer*; "Shad Daze" in *Angel City Review*; "Annealed" in *Meridian*; "Spawning Season" in *North Carolina Literary Review*; "Azimuth and Altitude" in *Inkwell*; "Proof of Me" in *Eleven-Eleven Journal*; "The Green Monster" in *Smokelong Quarterly*; "The Duck Walk" in *Phoebe Journal*; "RE: Division Unification" in *Swink*; "Evisceration Line" in *Keyhole*; "Freezer Burn" in *Little Patuxent Review*; "Verbindung Durch Angst" in *The MacGuffin*; and "Heirloom" in *The Dead Mule School for Southern Literature* and "Object Lessons" in *The Southern Literary Review*.

For ordering information, please contact:
Ingram Book Group
One Ingram Blvd.
La Vergne, TN 37086
(800) 937-8000
orders@ingrambook.com

For media and event inquiries, please visit:
www.newamericanpress.com

CONTENTS

RECORD

STITCH

VACUUM

CROWN

MARKET

"All things are delicately interconnected."

Jenny Holzer

"Every pattern piece bears markings that together
constitute a pattern 'sign language,' indispensable to accuracy
at every stage—layout and cutting, joining of sections, fitting
and adjustment. Note all symbols carefully;
each has special significance."

Reader's Digest Complete Guide to Sewing

RECORD

"When a new recording is made, the previous
recording will automatically be erased and only
the new recording will remain."

Panasonic RQ-2103 Operating Instructions

CADENCE

SOMETHING ATE A HOLE THROUGH THE OIL TANK, so we called Joey in from the pumps to fix it. The tank had been drained, mostly, but mostly never helped no one. Joey didn't have gloves, just some rubber goggles, and this one time nobody told him to go and get the good mask. He could've found the cat litter in the closet, could've poured it in first to absorb what we'd left in there, but he didn't do that either. It probably wouldn't have helped. Even with those goggles on, he would've seen the ember that strayed through the hole, the welding rod still pinched between his fingers, the little spark that built the flame that rocked us all to the back of the bay.

The body looks strange on fire. It's just everywhere at once, liquid and growing, with Joey tearing out toward the nasty patch of grass on Highway Eleven with flames eating through his skin. And we just stood there stupid, like disciples struck, outside the Gas 'N' Sip, helpless except for a woman waiting for an oil change who called

9-1-1 from our pay phone. But what were we supposed to do? He was gone, and we all knew it, except maybe for Mr. Andy Arlen, moving too late from behind his desk, belly-heavy in work boots, extinguisher in hand. The fire was out already. Joey was blind and smoldering with snuffed heat on that small strip of highway lawn, me kneeling nearby telling him the things he'd want to hear in his last few moments, as cars still pulled in to the station. And Mr. Goddamn Fucking Hero Arlen pushing through with his cherry-red tank, the pin pulled—it made me wish, as the foam hit and Joey screamed his last, that Mr. Arlen had stayed behind his goddamned desk. He stood over Joey holding the tank like he'd just taken the world's biggest pressurized piss. That's when I threw up.

IN ALL THE YEARS I KNEW HIM, Joey was never one to just let a subject be. And for the past month he'd been nonstop about his girl Becky in Basic. When she left for the Army he went on and on about the mix tape he'd made for her, the magazines he'd bought her, the fudge his mother made, the jumbo pack of Skittles he'd found at Sam's Club, the troll doll with camouflage hair and pants to match. He liked to tell me all about her "particular brand of fucking," as he'd called it, specialty moves of hers that I knew only too well. So well that I knew when he started to make stuff up. He didn't write many letters; he was more of a candy-and-flowers man. He'd sit at the station between pump calls and write a few I-miss-yous on yellow lined paper, or make me strum out cornball country songs on my guitar. And just last week he told me how the Skittles and the fudge and the mix tape and the rest of it was banned anyway.

"What she got, Billy Dice," he said, "was one good look at all the things I'd sent her. Then her sergeant took it away. Worse than me not sending it at all."

Becky has good features but bad skin that she tries to hide with beige makeup. She keeps at least three bottles of that stuff in her bathroom. I've seen it. Contour, she calls it. It works better at night, or in the dark, at bars a few towns over. Becky's barroom eyeliner makes you forget about those bottles of pancake in her bathroom, makes you forget how a close hug from her will more than likely leave a tan rash on your T-shirt. A few years back Becky was the Co-Captain Superstar Forward of the Lady Tigers, came close to a field hockey scoring record.

But the first time she took me home she was already over all that. She had a thread of green dental floss strung across her left breast, stuck to the nubs of her sweater, clinging like tinsel to the pilled part below her shoulder, and she gave me one of those hidden, rim-of-the-eye smiles when I asked about her hygiene technique.

"Gotta keep the girls plaque-free somehow," she said. She told me she'd started young in the bars, nabbing one of her big sister's IDs to get into Duck's Tavern when she was seventeen. No one ever called her on it, even though her picture was in all the papers that season. Ask me, that four-year jumpstart on bar life kept with her and there she was at twenty-four at the same bar looking at least thirty under all that makeup.

Becky's been writing to me since her first week at Basic, saying from the start how she wished she'd wrapped it up with Joey before she left. How she wants me instead of him. How the one thing Basic fails to train you for is what to do with the life you leave back in Mewborn, North Carolina. Last week she said Joey had one more letter coming, and then she'd be free for me, for real. She told me to watch for it, made me promise to talk to him if he brought it up. She said, "My sergeant says, 'The more you carry, the more you carry.' I don't have room for a troll doll, anyway."

And so I wasted the whole morning looking for clues in his face. At Burger King I waited for him to say something about her, because that was my cue, my lead-in to let him know his personal business with Becky was mine, too. I could see the folded note in the pocket of his T-shirt, the telltale border on the envelope beyond his Marlboros. But he just ate his burger and fries and asked about my next gig and talked about Friday's game at the high school like nothing had changed, like Becky was still scoring points in her plaid skirt and mouth guard, or crying in her pillow over confiscated Skittles. I waited for it all day and he said not a word, not a word until the spark hit that puddle of oil. Not until he was down on the ground with no face, me kneeling next to him—that's when he talked, right before Arlen came barreling through with his goddamn superman extinguisher. I heard him.

BECKY'S GOT A MONTH LEFT OF BASIC, and then it's off to Aberdeen for ordnance training. Between the training is two weeks at home. She's thinking about going Airborne so she can nab a Fort Bragg assignment, so there'd be but an hour between us. She picked ordnance, she said, because she loves dogs, even the bomb-sniffing ones. She's hinted more than once I should think about a move to Fayetteville. Even though she's in South Carolina and on her way to Maryland. Even though it's the Bragg soldiers they're shipping daily overseas to Kuwait. Even though I wasn't sure I wanted Becky in-the-Daylight. Becky out-of-Bars. Becky out-of-Bed. Becky Barker and Billy Dice. I wrote her as much using nicer words, said I wasn't sure I was worth jumping out of a plane for. But I said I'd talk to Joey if she talked to him first.

But then Joey died. I saw him tear across our lot with the welder still on. The oil tank scattered across the bay in white-hot pieces. Bits of it kicked into his skin, turned him in seconds to blue fire. He cooked the palms of his hands trying to pry the goggles from his face.

The rules change after a fuel tank explodes and eyelids burn away and tear ducts are gone and you're kneeling beside your best friend and his face and body have no skin. Becky would understand. In Basic they tell each other stories that end like this, best friends and fire and all. Knowing her, she'll listen to every track on that mix tape Joey made. She'll make me come pick her up at Fort Jackson and I'll have to hear it all the way home. And at some point, she'll loosen my grip from the stick shift and hold my hand in her lap and won't say a thing about what happened. She'll collar me with her silence and grief and guilt as "Tumbling Dice" moves through us, and that's when I'll know that I'm hers now, that this is the way she'll pull us into public. At Joey's funeral they'll play "I'll Be There for You" straight from the mixed tape and she'll appear in her respectable-looking dress uniform and claim her place as Grieving Girlfriend, and I'll be the Grieving Best Friend giving a show-stopping "He Stopped Loving Her Today" tribute at the church and his parents will be real nice to both of us, and won't it make sense to everyone for us to find comfort together in our loss? It's just what he would have wanted, she'll tell me, me finishing with her what Joey could not. Becky and Billy Dice. And how cheap would it be to tell her what a farce that mix tape really is, how Joey borrowed more than half of my tape collection and then used my double cassette boom box to make it? Let him have the mix tape. It's not worth upstaging someone after they're dead.

Which is why she won't ask what we talked about. Which is why I won't tell her that when I knelt by Joey and told him about Becky in her tall black boots, marching across a swamp in South Carolina, clutching a map, finding a coordinate, on her way back to him, Arlen almost there with the extinguisher, I swear I heard him say it. "I know, Billy," he said. "I know."

And what do I know? It was nobody's fault. Even when I thought about what might happen down the line, to her out there and Joey here and me in between, I saw it all working itself out. I didn't see myself looking at what's left of Joey. I didn't see me losing him and her getting me. I still don't see it.

THE GHOST RIDER

HARDLY NO ONE OUTSIDE NASHVILLE had ever heard of Billy Dice's All-Stars until last night, when our drummer, Marty Marshall, fell through the plate glass window down at Clyde's Country Corner. People these days always got their cameras out so we figure the more they film Billy Dice and us All-Stars, the better we look, and the better we look, the more they'll tip. So when we cleared the stage for Marty to hit his mega solo during "Ghost Riders in the Sky," he tilted back on the hind leg of his tripod stool and rose up, arcing his arms for a double-cymbal shimmer to close it out, and that was it: a YouTube sensation born within the hour. The whole world—or, eventually, 360,000 of us—watched as he crashed back onto the massive window behind him, tumbling in a glitter glass shatter out onto the street, taking the neon Bud Light sign with him, and toppling a handful of Stetson-toting tourist girls in their Daisy Dukes and nine-hundred-dollar boots like a strike in a bowling alley. They mostly darted out of Marty's way as he tumbled down, screeching the screech of a viral Internet sensation, and, still screeching, stuck their phones into Marty's face as he lay there on the sidewalk. And if that wasn't bad enough, Billy Dice poked his head out the window after Marty, his vocal mike still looped into the sound system and said, with laser-precision timing, "I was just thinking that drum was a hair too loud." When Billy Dice heard himself amplified through the din as laughter erupted, he got decent. "Hey, Marty, you all right?" just as the bouncer cleared the huddled filming-phone crowd and made way for the on-call medics.

As far as tragedies go, you couldn't have planned it any better. Marty turned out all right, in spite of everything—the screeching tourist cowgirls actually helped break his fall. After the medics checked Marty's vitals, they stood him up, brushed the excess glass off his vest, and sent him back inside to finish the set.

"A real, card-carrying union dude," Billy Dice said later, of Marty, between sips of whiskey.

"Got to get paid, man," Marty said to his beer.

Marty got all the attention that night, but I had my own little breakthrough playing out during the show that, thank God, no one knew to look for or see, unless of course you were Billy Dice, who could read a crowd better than Jesus, and when he saw Sage in it, could tell from the look on her face to steer the hell clear. Even when Benny brought round the tips bucket, he avoided Sage, and instead offered her a pleasant hat tilt as she guarded the portable ATM machine near the entrance, arms folded, staring me down, pressing an unlit smoke between her lips as I played busier and faster than I ever had. I chose not to look at her too much. Might as well give her a show, let her know what I'm worth.

Sage's unlit cigarette was her "compromise on this fucking smoking ban," she'd said after the bars down Broadway turned into family-friendly non-smoking venues. Another sign, to her at least, that the city had sold out to the cultural kudzu of the Country Music Association. Pain in the ass or not, she knew her shit, and plugged in for a solo set with her daddy's Martin whenever she could and people for once quit running their mouths to stop and listen. She was a powerhouse in her own right—on stage, in bed, in person—and thank god she didn't carry a phone, if for no other reason that it meant I'd never receive the torrent of texts that materialized in actual, real life complaints every time we met: where's my rent money? You'll pop over after your set, right? You know, this baby's yours, so when you gonna start acting like a Daddy?

I'm barely twenty-one, so Daddy is the last thing I need to be called right now, and most of our nights together are me telling her as much, tossing her a few twenties from my share of the tip jar to keep her happy. "Happy enough is different than happy," she'd say, quoting a line from one of her songs, and making sure I knew she was expecting me to stop by later, after we finished out at Clyde's. I rarely did. Well, sometimes I did. Often enough, I guess, for her to get the idea that staying over meant something more than a warm bed that wasn't a shared pullout sofa with Benny, and long arms and soft mouth and a fridge of food and hot shower. Somehow, she got the idea that if one was *actually* on the way, I'd volunteer to stop the world, put down my guitar, and make room for it. But something tonight with her was different. I could feel her smolder as I walked my fingers up and down the neck of my Telecaster, taking my cues from Billy Dice. The melody is predictable enough on these old standards that your fingers do all the work, leaving time for your brain, when it wasn't contemplating the likely arrival of a swaddle-clothed tot drooling on the fringe of your favorite Western shirt and the angry musician it would one day call Mama, to take in the crowd—a flirty band of Brazilian dudes; road trippers fresh off a blues night on Beale Street, assessing the two cities and their sounds as though they were in charge of them; a few regulars and a handful of tourists who actually eat those godawful fried baloney sandwiches; the overeager divorcée first dates, overdressed and sitting way up front like teenagers, hell-bent on having a good time; the line-dancing retirees clumsily keeping rhythm with their twists and turns. Say what you will about this gig—and Sage had a lot to say about it, that I was wasting my time on these old hat standards and this two-bit band—it makes people happy. We're not fifty steps from the Ryman but if you can throw basically the same party almost every night and folks still show regular as the tide, you're doing something right.

Except if you're me, and except if, as my solo ends and Marty's begins, Sage hovers toward the stage and leans in to yell something in my ear just as Marty tumbles through the window. All you see on the YouTube video is someone from the floor beckoning to the guitarist as Marty blows up the stage with his percussive energy, rattling through snare and bass and cymbal, making his own Outlaw sound snap alive, putting the "cow" in cowboy songs. And what was it that Sage shouts to me as Marty rises and plows through the window? "There's no more baby," she yells, for the whole stage to hear, although only I heard it. But Marty's ill-timed crash distracts me, and instead of looking into Sage's hazel eyes to see if she meant what she said, and what that meant for us if it was true, I whip around to catch Marty busting through the window, ass-first, and when I turn back toward Sage, she is gone.

Like the dog in the pony show, I couldn't just leave Clyde's and go after her. We had the gig 'til one, and we were only about halfway in, and I wouldn't get paid unless, like Marty, I stuck it out. During break, I stood hangdog outside Clyde's amid the shattered glass, the neon beer sign dangling above my head, the kaleidoscope of fairway lights from above and across the street blinking and reflecting in the shards our bouncer failed to sweep up, wondering what Sage meant, beyond the obvious. There's no more baby—Am I off the hook? Was there ever a baby? Did she finally figure out it was someone else's, or worse, did she know in her heart it was mine but knew deep down—as I did—that I wouldn't be able to handle it?

"That's some tumble," Billy Dice said, appearing at my side, pulling on his beer.

"No doubt," I said, trying to tamp down my thought spiral. Billy Dice was one of those ageless-but-ancient All-In types, the kind of guy who's seen it all, who needs you to say his whole name, as if he was a brand of himself. But "All-In" also meant that, based on what he saw, he'd corral you and your personal problems like a fucking border collie.

"Sage sure seemed agitated tonight," he said, leaning in. Fishing. Billy Dice knows better than to pry, but this was his way of letting me know he was open, if I was. All-In. I was not.

"Sage is always agitated," I said. "Looks like she got something else to agitate her tonight besides me."

"No doubt," Billy Dice said. Gaggles of drunkards cavorted down Broadway, hop-galloping in a sprawling gait toward us. "Are you the drummer who fell out the window?" one asked.

"Yes," Billy Dice and I said in unison. We cheersed our beer to each other, and then to the revelers, who cheersed back, took a few photos of the broken window, and flocked inside. These folks smelled like money and we both knew it.

"Time for work, babyface," Billy Dice said.

We came back strong off the break, all told, and rattled the crowd—the late-arriving drunkards proved as lucrative as we'd hoped—and that night we eased in a good $200 each. Still, the air-conditioning at Clyde's got all fucked up, on account of the broken window. So there I was during the gig, my body clammy from the indoor-outdoor climate war playing out on the stage, pit stains drenching my sides, unsurprised when the whole aircon overheated and shorted out our sound system in the middle of "The Whiskey Ain't Workin'." We were fine with it, really: an impromptu break for us while Billy Dice, with his ancient Epiphone (I always thought he could do better, but he swore by it) started in on an acoustic solo set that brought out all the slow dancer sweethearts, the old ladies and their gents, a few loners swept off their feet by some of the more gallant Brazilians. It was sweet, people touching, smiling, strangers moving in a swaying sync even as old Mr. Clyde himself emerged from wherever he counts his coins and flipped the circuits himself, right under the "Hank You" bumper sticker and a paper fan of Johnny Cash flipping the bird. Benny and I stepped out at one point for a smoke, when Katie came by and made an arrangement with Benny to come by our place when she got off shift.

"You know what that means," Benny said. What it meant was that I had to find someplace else to crash. Our room was just that: a room, and no one would want to witness the whatever that goes on between Benny and Katie. "You good with it?"

I nodded, pulled the last drag off my smoke, thinking maybe Sage would stroll by. She sometimes walked her German shepherd on Broadway, passing through the neon glamour of the strip, scouting out which bar she'd play at next. She usually got a haul of shows—just her and her guitar, a singer-songwriter just like the rest of us who came here to make it big, and treated her whole life like it was an audition, figuring she'd have that "right place, right time" moment at the Bluebird and some A&R guy would hear her song and sell it—"or, at the very least my soul," as she'd say—to Shania Twain or Taylor Swift or Emmylou Harris and then she could go off and have all the babies she wanted.

DURING MY BREAK, I rang up her house, but there was no answer. And after the set, too. And few times between back-pats to Marty, as his inbox filled with the link to the viral video and a slew of comments. Benny left as soon as he packed his bass and, by all logic, was by then in the throes of what-have-you with Katie on our pullout.

"Lucky dude, Benny is," Billy Dice said.

"Hey, send me that video," I said, leaning over Marty's shoulder to get a glimpse. I could see Sage's silhouette in the frame, and wanted to watch it in private.

"Hell, Quinn, I never took you for a Facebooker," Marty said, laughing, and we struggled like two idiots for almost ten minutes getting the spelling of my name right, where the hell to find the "at" symbol, and all that. As soon as I left the bar—"Take good care of that girl!" Billy Dice warned—I dug up my old email address to find the link to see what a few thousand people had (so far) seen but none of them knew to look for.

I left Broadway as soon as I could, toward the darker stretches of the city, where the sloping streets at night look nearly the same. Off Broadway, this late, everything looks drab, the beggars that roam these streets are more desperate and daring, unlike the dude who sits outside the T-Shirt shop with a cardboard sign "Smile if you Masturbate" that nabs him a few more bucks each night just for the laugh. Some folks claim a bench, or an old car in a dark parking lot. Others pitch incongruously bright camper's tents in an impromptu homeless city just below the I-24 overpass. Some hawk their guitars or harps or what have you, just to eat, while others keep their instruments buried in backyards or parks, like some dog protective of a bone no one else wants.

Weirdly, I felt that way about watching the clip. I actually waited 'til the street was clear before pressing play. In the video, the cameraman catches Sage in silhouette, hands clapped over her ears during Marty's solo, taking the edge off (the drum was, as Billy Dice said, too loud). Then she glances back, almost to the tourist cameraman, with a "watch this" confidence in her shoulders, in the way her corkscrew curls shine spaniel-like in the light as she approaches the stage. She wears green. Then her long bronze arm waves me over, swoops up toward my ear, delivering news in a whisper-gesture that I know is a barroom yell, as my fingers damp my strings, leaning over, leading with my non-monitor ear, and give her a tight smile that raises my eyebrows just as Marty rises and falls. Then Sage is out-the-door gone.

WITH MY GIG BAG STRAPPED TO MY BACK LIKE A BACKPACK, I kept walking and playing the clip when, finally, I saw it. In the split moment that I turn my head toward the window crash, and Sage darts off, my eye automatically draws up to the action of the crash on screen. There's something seductive about watching a man fall through a window, and your eye can't but help to focus on it, even when it's looking for something else. But if you keep your eye trained on Sage, you'll see that she flings onto the stage a folded-up piece of paper before she takes off. By the time she's gone, I unknowingly step on missing puzzle piece like an idiot and play out the rest of "Ramblin' Man."Fuck. A note. How did I not see it?

When I looked up from my screen and the bright spots hazing my eyeballs faded, I realized I was in front of her apartment building. It was well past two. The lights were out. I have stuff at her house, but I never claimed to actually live-live there. Maybe that was part of the problem. I wouldn't commit to her, or to anyone, except the band, and even that proved hard at times. Billy Dice always says any one of us is one bad break away from sleeping on a bench, or busking for a bus ticket home to North Carolina, which is why we got to take care of each other. I sat on the bench, thinking of the note, deciding what to do. I'm certain the barmaid swept it up minutes after our set ended. As the band talked over a beer at the bar, I literally watched her push the broom across the stage, brush the crap into a dustpan, and toss it all in the trash.

"Hey, man, got anything on you?"

"What?" I said, eyes still glazed from my phone glare. Some kid in a hoodie, gaunt face, looking cold even though it was May. Feeling both flush and unlucky, I tossed him a cigarette and a fiver I kept in my back pocket. "God bless, man," I said. That's when he hurled himself at me with a sharp little fist and nailed me in the eye.

"What the fuck?" I yelled, as he darted off down the street. So much for luck. Just wanted some human contact. I guess. Fucker.

I took the pulsing of my eye as a sign that I needed to at least tap on Sage's window. Maybe she had a cold cloth. Or a story to tell. Or a fucking sandwich that didn't include baloney. But my gut told me it was a bad idea, that I should just claim the bench and maybe she'll see me in the morning when she takes Shepard for a walk, unlit smoke hanging from her lip, and understand. And as I laid down, I could feel me standing outside myself, calling out Chickenshit. The image of me mocking myself, making chicken wings and cackling like a third grader would not leave my mind, so I got up and crept toward Sage's window. Before I could even tap, Shepard's snout emerged, his glowing eyes appearing in my reflection, followed by a sharp bark and, beyond the dog, an empty, made-up bed. Shep continued to bark like he didn't know me. I didn't wait around to see whether he'd actually bust through the glass and bite my ass, or what Sage would do if she was home and our eyes met through the window, she thinking I knew what was on that sheet of paper, or what it might mean if I told her how empty I felt, thinking about the idea of there being no baby now that there was no baby, and would it even make a difference to her? Because it made a difference to me.

The only thing left to do, I decided, was to track down the note, so I hauled off back to Broadway. The strip was dark, the streets still filled with garbage bags, even as the team of sanitation workers rolled down Broadway, leaving a sour trash swine smell in their wake, hauling up bag after black plastic bag of things left in the aftermath of a good time. The string of neon signs rested in the silence and dark sky and I realized I hadn't been down here and sober enough to notice how dingy everything looked without their glow and shine luring you in. Only the Nudie's Honky Tonk sign glowed on, no doubt the accident of a sloppy night manager, and so the curvy cowgirl in short shorts and spurs kept trying to lasso me in from across the street, and I thought back to Sage's empty bed and where she might be.

As I ARRIVED BACK TO CLYDE'S, I realized what I came for might just be on the street in a black plastic bag. I tucked my guitar away in the doorway, got on my haunches, and dug in. The broken window was flimsily protected by a stretch of yellow police tape—to fix it would take 'til at least Tuesday, Billy Dice said earlier, and wouldn't you know, Mr. Clyde himself was on stage dozing, propped up on two chairs, gut heavy slumped to one side, pistol hooked into the crook of his folded arms, guarding the bar.

I don't know if you've ever had to go through someone else's trash—going through your own is bad enough—but picking around in what thousands of drunk people in a single night literally wanted to get rid of, with a single streetlight and a glowing Lasso Gal across the strip, ain't fun. How many foam cartons, shards of glass, cigarette boxes and butts, someone's throw-up, napkins with stains from who knows what, stubs and ash like ghastly confetti, used tissues, gnawed-on chapstick, half-eaten sandwiches, empty bags of chips, a few torn-up dollars, fucking diapers, a carton of warm milk threatening to burst, rotten baloney, and shards of glass I sifted through to find one of my guitar picks and the folded-up note, wet from the muck at the bottom of the bag.

I held up the note to the light of the Nudie girl, gut quivering like

I could puke, just as the trashmen rolled through, and laughed at me crouching in shit.

"What you lose, boy?" one called from the back part of the truck. "Your hotel key?"

"Fuck you," I said. Did I look like some fucking tourist?

"Lost something," another joked, hauling up bags two at a time. "His mind, maybe?"

"Hey, ain't this the bar where…" the guy pulled out his phone. "This is where that drummer fell through the window!" Jeezus. The Ghost of Marty rides again. As they watched and hooted through the video, I unfolded the note. It looked like something a high schooler would toss across a classroom. Was it a letter? An ultrasound? But as I unfolded the paper, I could see it wasn't a handwritten declaration, or ultrasound photos, or even a breakup note. It was a typed-up copy of a contract with Third Man Records for Sage's first 7-inch record featuring "Happy Enough."

"What's going on here?" Clyde barked from the window. We all three darted our faces up to Clyde. "Quinn, what you doing down there?"

"Lost something on stage, Mr. Clyde," I said, folding the note and slipping it into my front pocket. I held up the guitar pick. The sanitation workers moved on, their motor rumble and tail lights the only other sign of life on the street.

"Rough night," Clyde said.

"You bet, sir," I said.

"Come 'round, I'll unlock the door," he said. He edged his way down the stage steps, side-stepping like a crab. The contract burned on my hip like a sterno flare—a contract? What was Sage thinking, tossing her news at me on stage? I imagined her at some sky-high Third Man condo party, and for once wished she had a cellphone. I wanted to track her down, but Clyde had summonsed me. The bloom of his body odor greeted me as I grabbed my guitar and walked in.

"Jeezus, boy, you stink," he said. He hit a few lights and found an old Loretta Lynn cassette and popped it on. The sound system designed for the Billy Dice All-Stars now carried the great-godmother of country.

"Hey, I got a joke for you," Clyde said, belching out the last of his beer. He fixed us up two George Dickels neat. Just as I needed.

"What do you call a guitarist with no girlfriend?" he asked.

Another one of those old-saw bullshit musician jokes. "Homeless," I said, cutting him off at the pass.

Clyde let out a jackass laugh, forcing in me a cracked smile. "Can't pull one on you!" he said.

"You have no idea," I said.

The Dickel was smooth enough, given the circumstances. I never really talked to Clyde before, one on one, so we let Loretta's twang fill the quiet between us.

"Talk about homeless," Clyde said, nodding up at the line of posters, "you know about George Jones, back in the late 70s? Lived out of his car, right up here a block or two. Liquid diet. Kept an old cardboard cutout of Hank Williams in the front seat just to have someone to talk to," he said.

"I guess Tammy was long gone," I said.

"You bet she was," he said. He switched the tape to Golden Ring. "Man, he weighed no more than 100 pounds at the time. We'd watch him stumbling 'round the strip looking for his next gig, showing up two hours late, if at all. Scary shit. I'd give anything to know what ole Possum said to Cardboard Hank." As we listened to George and Tammy going at it on the cassette, it hit me that Sage and I never actually played a song together. I got up to leave.

"Hey, you seen Martin's crash video?" he said.

"I seen a lot in my time," I said. I rocked on my stool, itching to clear out. What would we sing?

He laughed. "You can't be more than twenty, right?"

I gave him a half smile, my mind back on the contract. I really wanted to call Sage again, ask her about a duet sometime—maybe "Baby Ride Easy"?—but it was rounding past three, and all I could do was drink my Dickel and stew, listening to Clyde yaw on about George

Jones riding his lawnmower to the liquor store after Tammy hid the car keys, as he switched tapes to Twitty, then Porter and Dolly, then Merle.

"So tell me why you come here in the middle of the night with a black eye going through the trash? This ain't about no bullshit about a lost guitar pick," he said.

I forgot about my eye. That little shit. The bottom of the glass was closer than it appeared. I sucked down the last of it and focused in on Norm Hamlet's loopy pedal steel whine its way through "I Never Go Around Mirrors." I pictured Sage's empty bed and her not-so-friendly shepherd. Her gold star contract. I settled on an answer.

"Girl trouble," I said.

"What you got with girl trouble? Handsome guy like you. Think they'd be lining up and paying for the privilege," he said, filling my cup. "You want girl trouble, try this on for size." He leaned in from across the bar.

"Yesterday morning, I get a call from a lady friend come up in her RV from Texas, and did I have room in my driveway for her van? 'How long is it?' I asked. She said 'bout 36 feet.'" He started wiping down the counter, revving his storytelling engine.

"Well, I had no way to measure the driveway, but I figure, I'm about six feet tall, and she's waiting on me to let her know how long my, er, driveway, is, but I'm in my underwear. So I figure there's no one come around that early, so I plan to lay myself down, end to end, to measure the driveway. And no sooner do I hit the pavement does a goddamn cop car come by and stop when he sees me supine in the middle of the driveway in my goddamn underwear. And then he recognizes me and says, 'Sorry to bother you, Mr. Clyde, my apologies.' But the smirk's still in his eyes." He tossed his dishrag in the corner and downed his whiskey in a single gulp.

"What the hell do you say to that? The shit you go through these days just to get laid. Enjoy it now, kid, while you can. Speaking of…" He checked his glowing phone. "That RV gal's calling me right now." He stood up to leave, and nudged the bottle of Dickel toward me. "I'm gonna take this call. Could you man the window?"

I had nowhere else to go—Benny was probably dozing by now on the pullout, with or without Katie, Sage's place was definitely out. I had no car and no life-sized cardboard of George Jones to talk to, so why the hell not? Clyde crab-walked up the stairs to his office with a hushed "y'ello, honey," into his phone, so I took to the stage, awaiting ambush, swilling from the whiskey bottle, and settled in on the twin chairs, contemplating Clyde without his hat on, without his pants. Wondering if I'd ever literally lay myself down like that for someone else and what that would look like. I laughed aloud. Wait'll Sage hears this, I thought. And then stopped short. Fuck. The contract.

I pulled the contract from the back pocket of my jeans. It was even more damp now from me sweating on the pleather barstool for the past half-hour. The contract was solid. The indie label made instant darlings out of people like us, and it would take Sage places, book her big venues, opening for Margo Price or whoever, way beyond this piss-ant Broadway scene, to say nothing of the money that would surely follow. The bigger thing she wanted—beyond whatever it was she once wanted with me—was happening for her. The contract said it all. The contract said, Fuck you, Quinn.

I stood up and crumpled the paper, then hurled it through the window past an airbrushed poster of a demure Kitty Wells in a tiara and the bird-flipping Cash. The night sky had dimmed to gray, a time when even the ghosts on the street quit their wandering and settle in somewhere. Maybe I'd find that parking lot where George Jones lived out of his car. Or maybe Sage was home by now. Maybe I'd try the bench outside her apartment, play a song or two on my guitar, and see what happens next. I tried the door, but Clyde had bolted it shut. I glanced toward his office. It was the window or nothing. I tore down the yellow police tape, letting a half dozen ribbons flutter to the stage, then slid my gig bag through the jagged window. The glowing Nudie girl and her golden lasso kept her wink on me in the dim gray morning as I picked my way past the glass shards, gathered up my gig bag, and walked on down the dirty, sleeping street, ignoring more than just the gnaw in my stomach.

SPAWNING SEASON

Eavesdropping on the private lives of fish and insects for the past twenty years had convinced Ted Murphy that he was never alone. Every summer, Murphy would lie in a field or boat somewhere with his microphone and headset, collecting data, listening for signs of life and love. He was never disappointed. Some nights he caught the whirring screech of the male cicada. At other times, on the shores of the Neuse River, he'd hone in on the peculiar boops of the sea trout or the red drum. And in the background, if he listened carefully, he could hear much more than that: the murmured march of ants underground or the frazzled buzz of the mosquito. Sometimes the rush of wind would chafe the surface of the calm estuary and he would take in that, too. Listening to the chatter through the headset made the world seem full and rich, amplified and isolated, all at once. On occasion, out in a field at dusk, someone would find him. Usually, it was a lone man and his unleashed dog. Other times, a few jar-clutching children on the hunt for fireflies. He was never surprised. Footfalls have a way of interrupting the natural flow and swish of wind, especially in a field, and the microphone could cue him in better than any bloodhound. Something is always there to keep you company, Murphy believed, should you care to listen.

He tried to explain all of this one day to Florine Finch, the biology department secretary at Mewborn College. Before she delivered the bees to his office, Murphy had never paid her much attention, although he wasn't blind to her charms. Every time he entered the department office for a package or an appointment, her head would turn at a perfect ninety-degree angle, her smile ready, determined to accommodate. When she typed, which was often, her spine straightened and her breasts would somehow angle up, trapped by wooly sweaters, which she wore even in the summer. On account of the air-conditioning, she'd say. Her left hand winked bright with jewels; he had heard she was getting married.

When the last of the students cleared out for the summer, Murphy would stop by the office nearly every day to see if his kitchen bees had arrived. He had never really set out to become a keeper of bees, and how he came to have a hive happened as a kind of a mistake to begin with. After a while, he found that he rather liked the hymenoptera order, he liked their busyness and sense of purpose, even after the swarming debacle back in April. One afternoon in June, Murphy heard a rhythmic click and buzz in the hallway. It grew louder and stopped in front of the door to his office. There he found Florine Finch in the hall holding a bee box from the Beeline Apiary in Medina, Ohio.

"Well, aren't you nice, lugging those bees up two flights of stairs for me?" Murphy said. "You must have known how bad I wanted 'em."

Florine didn't look happy. Her lipstick had smudged and her whole face seemed ridged with worry. "You've been on the phone awhile, right?" Florine said. She was out of breath. "I've been calling all day. I just couldn't keep a box of bees in my office any longer. They're so… loud." She smiled in that sad, southern way. Murphy knew that look. He used to see it in his mother all the time back in Tennessee. All teeth, no eyes. Murphy found his phone under a shuffle of papers, apologized, and put it back on the hook.

"Those bees can buzz, can't they? There's about twenty thousand in there. An entire hive," he said. "With queen. For my kitchen bees."

She held the buzzing box with the tips of her fingers, as though it might explode.

"Twenty thousand...kitchen...bees?"

"Yeah. There was a mutiny a few months back? The workers reared up, killed the queen and swarmed to a tree in my yard. The others who stayed are all outta whack. The hive is a mess. I'll go right now to get these gals in there."

Florine looked skeptical as she wrestled with the box. Her narrow feet shifted in little pink sandals. He wondered how she managed to stand upright with all that height. Is this the source of the clicking noise? Could she run in those things?

"You had a beehive in your kitchen? With real bees?" she asked.

He shook his head, snapping out of the spell of her feet.

"What other kind of beehive is there?" he said.

Florine looked thoughtful for a moment. "Well, there's the hairstyle," she said, gesturing to the bun atop her head. Intrigued, he raised an eyebrow. He had not guessed her to be so funny. Beehive, indeed.

"But I have never heard of bees in a kitchen," she said.

"Right, right," he said. He supposed it did sound a bit strange. "I was gone from my house for a month or so, and when I got back, my kitchen was just floating with bees. Turns out they had made up a hive in the corner cabinet, above the sink."

"What did you do with the hive?"

"I kept them there for a while and left out a sugar solution. They have to eat, right? But the hive grew and there were a lot, I mean, a lot of bees. Did you know most bees are female? They hardly have use for the males, save for the queen. Boy, they're fun to watch."

Florine shifted the box from one hip to the other.

"Did you call an exterminator?"

"Naw, I wouldn't do that. I didn't want them dead," he said. "When it got warm, I built them a little bee hut, a super. I smoked 'em out and took a scraper to their hive. So when they were good and calm, I brought 'em outside, took the honey, and that was that."

"So, you gave secondhand smoke to bees, then took their honey?" she asked.

"Hell, they ate my sugar. I considered it their rent for six months. I'll bring you some."

"Isn't that dangerous? Won't they get cancer, or something? From the smoke?"

"Naw. Smoke calms bees. And most insects got a good instinct about people. They can feel your intentions. Plus, I was wearing a net and some gloves, so..."

Florine shifted the box away from her hip, as though she suddenly remembered what was in it.

"Could you please take this? Now?" That southern smile again. He glanced at her hand when he took the box. The engagement ring was gone. He was going to say something, but then he noticed Florine looking around, taking in the particulars of his office. Her head turned in that precise angle, one degree at a time, like the second hand on a clock.

Murphy knew he didn't keep the tidiest office, but in his defense, he had been at Mewborn College for twenty years. He liked to collect things. That's what he did. He considered most of the insects he kept, piled in old pickle and jam jars, to be research. He studied all kinds of species for their mating habits. One day, cicadas, the next day, fish or ducks. Murphy could see her take in all his anthropology stuff, the endless search for significance in the Kula ring and the potlatch, then the human skeleton and fish bones and Maori shells. In the corner was the log-shaped didgeridoo that his ex-girlfriend Shelley had given him before he left Santa Cruz for North Carolina.

Florine's survey of his office stopped when her eyes fell upon his ponytail collection, just above his desk, amid the cardboard jewelry boxes for his butterflies and glass jars filled with dice. They hung in various lengths and girths, the evolution of their shine and shade marking the past 28 years. Every seven years, ever since his dad died, Murphy had cut his hair. He didn't mean any symbolism or anything when he first did it, but his mother insisted that he look presentable for the funeral in Memphis. Those were different times. Shelley was still around, for one thing. She studied warm climate eels. Murphy had just started his post-doc in Santa Cruz, so he chopped off his ponytail at the office before he headed out to Memphis and threw the tail in a shoebox. When he came to North Carolina, alone, (Shelley couldn't bear to leave her eels) and started to unpack, he came across the first ponytail and tacked it to the shelf above his desk. He counted it out on his fingers and realized it had been seven years since he had cut his hair. When he found the shears in another box, he cut off the second tail, and tacked it up next to the first. Murphy figured it was a little strange, but they felt more like bookmarks, or milestones, rather than long strands of rubber-bound protein.

"There's no real reason for those," Murphy said. "I just thought every seven years, I'd cut my hair." He stroked the ponytail now falling below his shoulders. It had been a healthy seven years, although he was sure there were a few more wiry whites mixed in this time than in the past. "I think I'll be ready to cut this one in the next few months."

Florine squinted as she inspected Murphy's ponytail. He obliged her, turning his head and shoulders so she could see it.

"It's like deciphering rings on a tree," Florine said. Her hand reached out to touch one of the tails, but then she stopped herself. "A dog's year, each one."

Murphy did a quick calculation in his head. "Actually, one human year equals seven dog years, so what you see here is um…196 dog years. That means I am a very old dog." Florine crossed her arms and looked at Murphy. He could tell she did not like to have her analogy messed with, even if it was, technically, inaccurate. Just then, Murphy spotted his didgeridoo in the corner of his office.

"You ever hear a didgeridoo?" Murphy asked Florine. "I'm a bit rusty, but check it out."

Murphy set down the box of bees and wrangled with the instrument until it stood waist high between them. He picked it up and started to blow. Instead of producing a deep, creamy echo, Murphy sputtered a hollow groaning noise that filled the room. Florine covered her ears. She shook her head when Murphy motioned for her to try it out.

"Keep practicing, professor," she said. Murphy felt warm, then wiped the spit from his lips. He set the didgeridoo down and in that moment of silence, the din of the bees grew louder. Florine waved at him and turned on her heel, one hundred and eighty degrees toward the door. Beehive hairdo. A dog's year. Keep practicing. He could hear her sandals echo down the hallway. She was amazing.

"I will," he called after her. "Have a good weekend."

THAT EVENING, AFTER HE INTRODUCED THE BEES TO THE WOODEN SUPER in the backyard and marked the queen with a big white dot, Murphy hitched up the rowboat trailer to his pickup and headed out to the estuary to listen to the spotted sea trout prepare to spawn at Rose Bay Creek, near the mouth of the Neuse River. Out past Mewborn, on the way to Little Washington, the highway shifts from a four-way freeway to a rinky-dink back road that carves through the dormant downtowns of Grimesland and Chocowinity. Out on the highway, mixed in with the run-down farmer's mansions and trailer parks, were acres of bright leaf tobacco, about a dozen churches, and the occasional doublewide strip joint. He drove by the Piggly Wiggly Plaza and saw on the marquee Gwaltney sausage for sale. He took in the advice of backlit signs from strip mall churches:

"What's missing in Ch __ch? UR!"

"Evolution is a Religion, not a science."

Murphy thought about that last one for a while as he headed east. You have to have faith that change is possible, he thought, that everything out there is guiding your mind toward new opportunities. Whether that kind of evolution was steeped in science or faith was beyond him. And maybe it didn't matter. He accelerated, cruising past the cotton fields just starting to gather their bolls. Soon, the air would be wispy with the haze of loosed cotton. In the fall, it looks like popcorn, sitting on a crisp brown star, an open palm offering a gauzy gift. Someday, Murphy would find the courage to pull over to the side of the road and fill the bed of his truck with fresh cotton. Maybe he would go to the art department, borrow a loom, and weave his own face cloth with it.

After he unloaded the boat, Murphy attached the hydrophone to his digital recorder and rowed out into the estuary's calm waters. When he found the right spot, he lay back, tethered by his anchor, pressed "record," and took in the songs of fish. He always found calm, watching the summer sky turn from pale blue to the color of carrots as the sun sank. The fish, under the dark cape of quiet, gathered underwater. Murphy could hear them begin with a few ticks and clicks and he closed his eyes and soon Florine Finch crept into his thoughts. He recalled her nervousness with the bee box, the peculiar glance at his didgeridoo. Her missing ring. "Keep practicing, professor," she had said. The way she spun on one heel of her pink sandal and left his office. Murphy drifted off to sleep in his boat as the taps and burps from the sea trout below mingled with the memory of pink lipstick at the corner of Florine's mouth. The kitchen bees and singing fish and Florine's hairstyle and hips blurred into the tones and sounds of the dark night along the Neuse.

MURPHY RETURNED HOME LATE FROM ROSE BAY CREEK, covered in red bumps from mosquito bites, and discovered the next morning that he had missed out on a good bit of data during his twilight nap. He had initially thought the chorus of spotted sea trout would climax just once, but as he took the recorder out with him on his morning run, he realized that those fish had been up to something more. Round two had happened, later in the night, and he had failed to catch it live. Listening to the recording during his jog, he could detect clicking sounds and an occasional sliding burp, and a gentle thump that bellowed like a heartbeat. The burp, produced by the fish's swim bladder, sounded like the low-pitched groan of an opened door. Usually, the larger leks happen in the early evening, but this one was out of step, a little later and louder.

Sometimes when he ran, Murphy wanted to close his eyes and rely on his imagined sonar instinct to keep him from falling off the curb. He tried it once and broke his glasses on a utility pole. Afterwards, he kept his eyes on the ground, the closest thing he could get to running blind without breaking his neck. Because of this, he almost didn't notice Florine—and it would have just killed him if he had run right past her—lugging a bag of trash to her curb. First, he heard clicking sounds, and then spotted the pink sandals, the same ones that had clouded his visions of fish grunts and crackles for the past twelve hours, and had lulled him to sleep during an unprecedented lek. Florine's beehive was gone, but her dark hair was tied back. He looked up from the click of her shoes into her southern smile.

"Hey, professor," she said.

"Hi Florine. Um, call me Ted," Murphy said. "Or Murphy. Everyone else does." He was a little short of breath and he scratched at the mosquito bites on his shoulder.

"Ted, then. Wow, those must really itch. Did the bees sting you?"

"Naw, they wouldn't do that. It was last night's skeeters. They sure did make a snack of me," he said. "I was on the boat and fell asleep and forgot my bug spray."

"You should be careful, you know. West Nile and all that," she said. "By the way, I was just looking at my garden. You must know something about bugs. Could you come look at this?"

"Of course," he said. Murphy never would have figured Florine for a gardener—those fine nails, the glittering stones in her ears. She wore pale pants that ended at her calves and a pink sweater top that matched her shoes.

"I found a glassy beetle in my garden. I can't imagine something this beautiful exists."

"Where is it?"

"Out back. I'll show you."

Murphy, still itching, followed her into the courtyard of apartments and onto her patio deck. There, in a bucket-sized terra cotta pot, stood a small green tomato plant. An iridescent beetle crawled up its fledgling stalk. Florine stooped low to the pot.

"Look at this. It's so beautiful; is it rare?" She looked up at him, looking for approval of her find. "It just looks like it's covered in dew. Every color out there, trapped in this beetle." It held the shape of a crystal ladybug, reflecting and absorbing light. "I mean, if a beetle like this were common knowledge, more people would know about it. Keep them as pets, right?"

Murphy hated to break her heart. These were the conmen of all the garden pests. They weren't worse than aphids, but they would certainly pose a problem for her tomato plant. The beetle's iridescence was the result of a bit of liquid lodged between its chitin cuticles. It turned colors when stressed, and if you decided to keep one, thinking you could preserve its beauty, it would turn black and hollow when it died. Murphy could tell she just loved the thing, and the last thing he would want to do to someone who's just discovered an insect that fascinates her is to tell her it's a bad one and then urge her to kill it. But he couldn't let Florine keep this thing without warning her. It would kill the plant.

"Looks like you got yourself a milkweed tortoise beetle, there. Pretty little pest, huh? You'd think it's the magic fairy cousin to the ladybug, but they're nothing but trouble," he said.

"This thing? It's so gorgeous, how could it harm anything?" Florine plucked it off the stalk, letting it run along the tip of her ring finger. It crawled toward her hand and paused, just past her knuckle. Her smile faded, and he caught the sparkle, and it brought him back to spring semester, the winking diamond that was now gone from her hand. Oh man, Murphy thought. This was one smart critter. Insects waste no time getting to the heart of things. Rattled by the pest going straight for Florine's ring finger, Murphy tried to shift her attention away from it, from what he guessed it was trying to tell them.

"It's just a milkweed tortoise beetle, a *Metriana bicolor*. No, sorry. It's a *Metriona bicolor...triona.* They're common around here, like houseflies or slugs, only prettier," he said. "And just as pesky, too. They'll tear your tomatoes apart."

"This is my first garden, so I wouldn't know," Florine said, murmuring at the beetle. The halves of its shell parted, and in an instant, it was gone, floating like a soap bubble, back toward Florine's one-plant garden. She looked like she was about to cry. Her nostrils expanded, and her face went deep red. Murphy didn't know what do except to keep talking about plants and pests.

"Well, if you keep these things hanging around, it'll probably be your last," he said. "Just spray the plants with soapy water, but only when you come home after work. You do it midday, or even in the morning, the sun will singe the soapy leaves."

"And what does the soap do?" Florine's redness subsided. She looked a little better. Interested, at least, in the soap idea.

"It gets in their spiracles, their breathing chambers. Insects breathe from their sides," he said, gesturing to his ribcage. "The soap mucks up the works." He looked at her, carefully at first, and then raised an eyebrow. He could tell she was really listening to him; there was an expression on her face that he saw when he was getting through to some of his best biology students. A little fun never hurt anyone, he thought. He looked around the patio, as if he was about to tell her a secret, letting her in on a conspiracy.

"Now, keep in mind, these aren't exactly the kinds of insects you'd want to eat. Butterflies, too, are a problem. All the colorful ones are," he said. "Too many alkaloids. It's practically poison... an insect's fair warning to stay the hell away."

Florine seemed unfazed by his effort to shock her with the idea of eating insects. Murphy knew them to be some of the most nutritious beings on the planet.

"What about slugs?" Florine asked. "Should slugs be avoided, professor?"

"It's probably not a good idea to eat slugs, but if you can dig up a few cicadas, well, I've got a stir-fry recipe for you," Murphy said.

Florine smiled. Murphy couldn't tell if she was interested or if she was just humoring him. The cicada stir-fry was actually quite good.

"I'll stop by your office to get it," she said. "I'll bring some bug spray for you, too." She noticed his headset. "Say, what are you listening to? A didgeridoo performance?"

"Check it out." He offered her one of the headphones. "Now that there's a lek. Female fish-wooing, basically," he said, listening in to the fish. The second lek of the evening was emerging just then. The clamoring of the sea trout grew louder with boops and clicks.

"A what?"

"A lek. That's when all the male species get together to bring out the female species. Like with fish, if there's just one or two weak ones singing out there, the females might not come out. But if they hear a loud, strong signal, they'll be more interested to see what's going on. For the males, it's just friendly competition, a serenade for the ladies."

"Wait. Fish make noise?" she asked.

"You bet they do. With their swim bladders. You got your oyster toadfish. Then there's the spotted sea trout, which is what you're listening to now," he said. "I've got recordings of red drum and weakfish, out near Ocracoke. You won't find them in the Neuse."

Florine adjusted the earphone. For a moment, their noses almost touched. "If scribbles could speak," she said, "this is what they would sound like."

"No, ma'am... it's communication. A fish serenade. They're all chattering down there with their little swim bladders, a chorus just waiting to spawn with the ladies," he said.

"I've never heard of anything like this," she said. "I thought you studied bugs, not fish."

"What I study is mating habits. Sexual dimorphism. This happens with tons of species. You've got your fiddler crab, the Tungara frog, the blue manakin, the hammer-headed bat, all the fish. Have you heard the buzz of a cicada? Only the males chirp like that. They're doing the same thing. Sperm is cheap, my friend. The fellas got to do something to stand out, right?"

"Kind of like the singles scene downtown," Florine said. She handed the headphone back to Murphy. "Do you ever feel alone out there, listening to fish all the time?"

"Lonely? No. Not at all. The entire world is full of life."

Florine shrugged. "I've been feeling lonely lately. It seems like you're alone with your work a lot. That's all. I wonder if you like it, or how you cope."

Murphy took a step backwards. "Well, I suppose I am alone out there," he said. He was unable to control the tone in his voice as he took another step away from her. "But it doesn't feel like work, so there's nothing to cope with. Every night, I go out to the field, or the waterfront, and I am surrounded by friends."

Florine looked confused. "I only wanted..."

"I am not lonely. Certainly not." Murphy couldn't stop his legs from trotting down the sidewalk, leaving Florine to contemplate glass beetles and the mating rituals of fish. How could she think he, of all people, was lonely? Why had she said that? He ran back to his house, making better time than usual, and covered himself in netting to check on the bees. As he scraped away the wax to get into their super, it struck him that he wanted Florine to join him that night in the field; that she'd said "alone" not "lonely." Darn. He should have inquired about the engagement ring when he had the chance. He wanted to let her know that he liked her pink shoes and that he wanted her to listen to marine nightlife with him along the Neuse. He wanted her.

THAT NIGHT, AS THE LUSTY CHORUS OF THE CICADA VIBRATED THROUGH the night, Murphy lay in the grass with his headset and microphone, listening for the click of her footfalls, thinking about the buzz of his didgeridoo. Maybe he would bring it along next time. As the sky grew dark, his inner dialogue replayed their conversations about loneliness and kitchen bees and beehive hairdos and the dating habits of spotted sea trout, eventually drowning out the gorgeous, familiar lull of the world outside.

THE SHIT BRANCH

Pa had been gone all winter.

It was Christmas night the last time we saw him: the old man in the foyer of our family home, booze-face flushed to red. Mom held a hand to her cheek to contain the sting from his slap.

"Don't tell me what to do," he'd said. Slurred, actually. Something about money. Something about mistletoe. He was in no condition to go anywhere, Mom said. She begged him not to. But of course he was going. Even he probably knew he'd already pushed beyond what passed for acceptable in the Burns household. There was no other option but Out.

Mom knew it. Pa knew it. Even with bottle of Jameson in his system, he still knew it. That's how smart he was. it, too. But we were too young then to know what words would matter to Pa in a near two-bottle state. To make him stop hitting Mom. To keep him from leaving when a storm was raging. And when he skipped the glass and swilled straight from the bottle, we knew we'd have an early bedtime. But that night, my kid brother Archie showed everyone who was the bravest of us three boys, who was truly mom's champion, when he dug out the Monopoly game from the pile under the tree and brought it into the foyer where the folks were having it out. Wylie and I hunched behind the tree as Archie held it, one-handed, like a pizza pie, a soldier in footie pajamas, and lifted the box between them.

"Hey, guys! Let's play a…" he'd said, just as the fake money and hotel shares and Community Chest cards and the dice and the little silver-plated sheep and racecar and thimble sprawled across the floor.

In the confusion of the cleanup, as everyone fell on hands and knees to pick up the silver-plated trinkets, the fake money, the hotels and houses, Pa made his exit into the snow-filled dark of the night.

We never saw him again.

Archie wailed for days, blamed his tears on the missing racecar. But we all knew better.

NOT ONLY HAD PA LEFT ON CHRISTMAS NIGHT, he did so in the middle of a Nor'easter boring down across New England. Pa liked to call these "Yankee Storms" on account of the statewide shutdown, as though snow was a conspiracy. A year later, during a science project for middle school, I learned that Nor'easter storms have a circular quality to how the tiny flakes fall, trapped in a pattern, like a shaken snow globe. For hours that night I stared out my window, watching the tumbling, rolling flakes pattern through the steady streetlight, hoping to see a dark figure barreling home through the world of white.

After Pa left, Mom called the cops, but it took two full days before they did anything about it. And it wasn't until the first big thaw two months later that they found him, stone frozen in a snowdrift, two blocks from our school. We passed that snow pile every day, played Fortress on it every afternoon, even though none of us felt much like playing. The more time we spent outdoors in the cold meant less time listening to Mom cry. She did little else in that winter-long stretch, the phone extension an arm's length away. When the phone did ring, she'd answer it on the half-ring, and we'd listen at her door, trying to catch from the tone of her voice if Pa was on the other end, or the police. We could always tell if it was the police or some business stuff because Mom's voice would shift into some weird pitch that made it sound like she was on TV, like she hadn't spent the past few weeks sobbing in a bathrobe. Other times it was Pa's folks calling long distance from North Carolina, or Pa's former boss at the plant, checking in. We didn't learn until later that Pa had been fired just before Christmas for drinking on the job.

Amazing where the mind moves in the absence of certainty, how it becomes convinced of the ugliest or strangest from among the available scenarios. After Mom turned out her bedroom light, we three boys would convene by the window in our bedroom, keeping watch, and try to reconstruct what might have happened, what probably happened, and why. I, for one, was convinced we'd get a postcard any day from the Florida Keys. I'd check the mail, even on Sundays, hoping my theory would prove right, hoping Pa would have written a note just to me, inviting me down there to join him in the sun.

We thought perhaps he'd actually made it down to Hugo's, his favorite bar—although the police reported otherwise.

"Maybe he meant to come back," Archie said, "but he got into a fight with a pack of alien ice bandits."

"I vote for a floozy in a convertible with chains on her tires," Wylie said.

"Maybe he crossed paths with the Abominable Snowman," Archie said.

Looking back, it was interesting how convinced Wylie and I were that Pa had up and left. After all, maybe he was sick of mom. Sick of us. Sick of the snow. Sick of the annual mistletoe operation. And our guessing game for his absence made us all look deeper into what was wrong with our family, why he would choose to leave us in the middle of the biggest storm to hit New England. Meanwhile, the police had no leads. And nothing arrived by mail. And, Mom soon discovered, the mistletoe cash was gone.

*

When he wasn't drunk, Pa was mostly all right. At dinner, he'd crack jokes about barflies and dumb blondes, midgets who play pianos, and howl along with Wolfman Jack on the radio. He showed us how to measure the perimeter of our backyard and let us take target practice on squirrels and tin cans. Wylie always got the shot, but I faked lousy aim, unwilling to advertise my unwillingness to shoot a squirrel. Sometimes in the summer, while Mom got dinner ready, Pa would pass a can of beer around the living room. We boys would sip at the cold, foamy bubbles and watch the Wheel of Fortune on TV, or a classic John Wayne flick, trying not to wince from the cheap, yeasty tang of Pabst Blue Ribbon. Sometimes Pa would complain about Pat Sajak's haircut. Other times, about the Pentecostals who held tent meetings in the vacant lot down the street. Or the women's libbers from Wellesley on their latest march, holding up traffic. Or any Northerner who'd bitch about how hot they were in eighty-degree weather. "Let 'em visit Eastern Carolina," Pa would say. "That'd teach 'em a thing or two about the heat." At Thanksgiving, we'd pile into the car and drive down to see Pa's folks in Mewborn. Granddaddy was an undertaker, so instead of visiting with family the Friday after Thanksgiving, Granddaddy and Meemaw Burns would go straight back to embalming bodies and running wakes like clockwork. Which was fine, because we had our own work to do out in the swamps— usually Mattamuskeet—hunting down the mistletoe in the "sick parts" of the forest.

We'd each be assigned tasks: Track, Shoot, or Catch.

Every year, as we tromped through the woods, armed with shotguns and knives and legions of black plastic garbage bags, watching the ducks on the lake convene in caucus, Pa would tell about mistletoe as though we'd never heard it before.

"The way I know it," Pa said, "we got mistletoe up there because some bird ate one of them white berries from some other tree, and then took a crap in this one." He turned around, his chin craning skyward, and pointed. "And that one, too. Look alive, Track."

"Yes, sir. There, Wylie," I said. "Shoot."

Wylie took aim with the Remington and missed.

"It ain't no moving target, boy. C'mon," Pa said. "Keep your eye shut. Get that thing in your sight, and get it down here." Wylie shot down a big clump of mistletoe on the third try. Archie—in the role of Catch—ran to get it. Pa continued.

"Mistletoe only shows up when the tree's on its way out," Pa would say. "One of the meanest parasites out there."

"Like tapeworm?" Archie would ask.

"More of an infestation. Like rats," Pa said. "Get this. The Germans? Call it the 'shit branch'. *Mistel.* And here in America, we can't quit kissing beneath it."

I could never shake from my mind the image of some girl kissing a turd on a stick as we hauled our catch out of the woods in trash bags, Santa Claus-style, and into the back of the station wagon. What didn't fit, Pa would secure on the roof beneath a bright blue tarp. The next morning, a Saturday, we'd drive north, take turns at rest stops, and Pa would always say, "Guard the shit branch, y'all."

We'd arrive home late Saturday and as soon as dawn hit Sunday morning, all five of us would be up and in operation. We boys would haul the bags of shit branch into the house and empty them, carefully, onto what seemed to be an acre's worth of old sheets that Ma had spread out across the kitchen. Pa would dig out massive spools of fake red velvet ribbon from Woolworth's, and tell us to find Ma's tape measure and scissors from her sewing cabinet.

"Cut the lengths on an angle about this long," he said, holding his palms about a foot apart. "Like this. Fold it in half, then on the angle, snip." While we boys cut the ribbon into forked-tongued ends, Pa would use a Bowie knife left over from his Vietnam days to cut the mistletoe into sprigs. Ma tied the bows. Together we made what had to be about a thousand sprigs of mistletoe, and Pa spent the next week roadside, selling off every last one for five dollars apiece. The pair of hand-lettered signs said it all:

Fresh-Caught Mistletoe: $5
Test: free (see attendant)

A few times a week, if my homework was done, I got to tag along with Pa. Turned out, in addition to his sign, and the cassette player that endlessly blared "Carol of the Bells," Pa had rigged up a sprig that dangled like a fishing pole line off the brim of his "Mistletoe Test Hat" and showed it off to every pretty lady who stopped in. Only one took him up on a kiss when I was around, a quick peck on the cheek, and you could tell she was just being nice. Even though everyone says from among the three sons I take after him most, I know Pa probably wasn't the handsomest of men, with his skin cracked in straight lines from nose to jowl, and his thick, paunchy cheeks. By Christmas Eve, nearly every last one of the sprigs sold, and Pa would give us boys each twenty dollars for our help. It wasn't until I was in college that I understood that mistletoe was the reason why we always had such flush Christmases, and why, after Pa disappeared with two thousand dollars in his wallet, they stopped. Who knew for how long that cash would keep our family afloat?

"Amazing the good money folks'll spend on a chance for a damn kiss," Pa would say, sucking on his Marlboro. "Happy Shit Branch, son."

Mom wouldn't let us see Pa in his casket. She said it was hard enough to see him in the morgue, his face blackened from frostbite, body mangled from the force of the snowplow. But of course we looked—how could we not? Alone at the funeral parlor, Mom talking to the director, surrounded by flowers, waiting for everyone to arrive. Three boys in love with gore? How could we not look?

We looked.

We barely spoke to the people who moved through the reception line. We huddled together at night in the same bed, eyes open and silent. We didn't sleep for a week.

Every once in a while, I'll think about that vacant lot, how we boys had played a full month on that snow pile, defending our territory from imaginary polar bears or ice vampires, as our father lay frozen within.

One time, Archie even peed right on it. Just stuck out his pecker and tried to write his name in the snow.

"I'm now an official member of the Yellow Snow League," he'd said. We held our noses and complained about the nasal pollution we'd suffered from his piss vapors. Archie gave a sinister laugh, and aimed his pecker toward us, and gave it another squirt. Nothing came out.

"Maybe a plow truck hit him," Archie said once, at breakfast, when mom was downstairs changing the wash. "Maybe he took a tumble somewhere and they plowed him in."

We dismissed Archie's snowplow theory at the time, along with the Abominable Snowman and Ice Alien Gang. But if Pa had been around to hear it, he would have given Archie the Best Guess prize, hands down. Because that's exactly what happened.

When they found him, the inner pockets of Pa's coat were stuffed with objects that could only be described as sentimental: a South of the Border family photo (all of us grinning in fake Mexican hats, mouths shaped into joyous "O's" because the photographer made us all say "taco"); a crushed up piece of mistletoe, with a half-dozen dried-up berries, attached by string to his ballcap; and the ugly-ass Shrinky-Dink Darth Vader keychain that Wylie had made him for Father's Day. And there was the fortune from our last Chinese takeout: "Find humor where you least expect it."

In Pa's clenched hand was the racecar from the damn Monopoly game. And in his wallet, two thousand dollars, cash. That Pa had been trapped dead in a snowdrift this whole time brought an odd relief to everyone, especially to Mom. Sure, he left the house that night mad and drunk with the snow falling and draping in endless frozen ribbons, upending our tiny lives. But at least we knew he wasn't quite ready to quit us. Not yet.

"Please note: A balanced tension (identical stitches both top and bottom) is usually only desirable for straight stitch construction sewing."

Singer 2263 Instruction Manual

HEIRLOOM

MAMA'S WATCH STOPPED LONG BEFORE SHE DIED. Its placid moon face stood cold against my ear, silent. I fingered its white, fake-leather strap, and with my thumb flipped the tongue of its gold-plated buckle. Along with everyone else, I pretended to ignore the smell of her death one flight up from the fanless kitchen. But my fingers kept finding their way to the watch, winding it up, willing the glass-trapped hands to move, the parts to tick.

"Anna, you gonna drink your tea there?" Clara asked. She wanted me to do something else with my hands, something to shift everyone's attention away from the TV. I set down the watch and took the tea. The alkaline tang of the bitter leaves greeted my mouth, barely masked by the half-bag of sugar.

Certainly, Clara had not set out the tea for me; nor the legions of casseroles and tubs of fried chicken from Parker's, the stretches of cakes and pastries on the countertop. I was glad of it. Six months earlier, these same throngs of aunts and cousins sat at our oval oak table, alongside Mama, sitting witness to me opening their gifts on behalf of the babies inside me that nobody wanted me to have, and that no one wanted me to get rid of.

"Love the sinner, hate the sin," Aunt Sarah said at least twice during that party. Cassidy Penelope and Clay were born a month later, twins, a full month early. But Clay was too tiny, couldn't take all the tubes and needles. We lost him after two weeks.

Now, sixteen of us stuffed in that sweltering kitchen, convening to mourn the death of my mother by watching Porter Wagoner reruns. No one spoke of Mama upstairs in her bed, or the stench cast throughout her house. No one ate after the men left for the bar, although my little cousins, Junie and Shirl, kept picking off the crispy skin from the drumsticks Clara set out. They'd strip the breading clean from the flesh and eat it, lick their salty fingers, and brush unseen crumbs from their lap, balling napkins in their greasy fists as though it never happened. I didn't touch the chicken, wouldn't, either, until they left. As the summer night grew dark, our lamp porch glowed gold. No one had turned it on; it had been on all day without our notice.

Shirl stripped a second chicken leg when Aunt Sarah barked over the din of the set, "Who's there?" toward the screen door, toward the hunched shouldered male form, peering into the house. The face appeared in relief from the porch light, casting color on sweaty cheekbones and a forehead pressed against the screen. His dark suit proved later to be russet in color, and he clutched a paper bag. I hadn't heard a knock; no one had. His left hand was poised mid-rap when Aunt Sarah spoke.

"About to knock," Mr. Burns said, in a smile that I'm sure pained him.

As the only undertaker in three counties, Mr. Burns had returned directly from his Florida holiday with a face so red from the sun he could barely smile in that sad, undertaker way. Still, he managed, "I'm sorry for your loss, all of you." You could see the white lines in his jowl when he stopped smiling and already flakes from his reddened dome of a scalp mingled with his wisp of a hairline.

"You're here now, and that's what matters," Clara said. She opened the refrigerator. "Would you like any cake?" As my aunts rose up to talk over, as they called it, "the situation upstairs," Clara brought out a store-bought red velvet. For all of her health issues, Mama died in her sleep: the good way, the best of ways. Everyone said so. No doctors or feeding tubes; no machine forcing air into your lungs, willing your heart to work; no unfamiliar setting to contend with when your soul finally released.

"She died at home, right where she wanted," Aunt Sarah said, for the dozenth time in so many hours, and, now, to Mr. Burns. "Right where she was."

All day I'd wanted to point out to my aunt her lack of logic. Because, isn't it true, that, even if Mama died walking down the street or up in a tree, she'd be "right where she was?" But I held my tongue and instead thought of my own baby girl sleeping upstairs. The baby lay one room over from her namesake grandmother. Each shrouded in sheets, and each sharing the same name: Cassidy Penelope. I picked up the watch and stretched out its strap, as I thought about the elder Cass, then the younger, feeling the tiny craters of the unused holes, the darkened indent where the fake gold clasp attached. One hole, three notches in, was larger and stretched out to accommodate Mama's thin wrist. She'd been sick for years, but in the past month or so took a turn for the worst. I tried on the watch. The circumference of my wrist was two holes bigger, and at least ten holes larger than Cassidy Penelope's. I know because I'd tried already to fasten the watch on the baby's wrist. Just to see.

"Give that here, Anna," Aunt Sarah said. "You'll break it."

"It's already broken," I said. "She wore the watch for years and it never worked."

"It worked at some point," Aunt Sarah said. "Else why would she wear it?" She reached across the table of cold food and grabbed at the watch. As though I were ten, not sixteen. I glanced at Clara, still talking business with the undertaker. My cousins for once quit stripping the skin off the fried chicken to see what I'd do.

"I should go check on the baby," I said. I stood, dangling the watch just beyond my aunt's meaty grasp, and left the room. As I started the stairs, I heard Aunt Sarah say, "Who takes a watch from a dead woman's wrist?" I let her comment pass, because it was partially true and because I knew not to sass my aunt in front of company. But I took each step double up the staircase, booming footfalls, demonstrating I was moving away from them, away from the drone of the television, from their hushed, angry voices, toward dear baby Cassidy.

THE HOUSE I GREW UP IN IS NEAR A CROSSING called Mewborn, North Carolina. Beyond the loblolly pine grove are acres of overgrown farmland and pecan trees and each spring generations of seeds sprout uninvited through the crabgrass and the burrowing tunnels crafted by voles and rabbits. When I was younger, I'd sometimes imagine dropping myself deep into one of those holes, Alice in Wonderland-style, and lose myself in their underground network. Not long after my Pa left us, when I was ten, Ma got sick. Even when she was feeling good in her body, her sickness took a toll on her mind. She forgot names or whether she'd left the stove on. She was not really the wandering type, one of those old ladies in bedclothes found out on the state highway. Thank goodness for that. But wandering's what killed her in the end, when one morning she went into little Cass's room to check on her and slipped. The doctors said she was fine, but she died in her sleep two days after the fall.

For years, I'd bound up the stairs and into Mama's room to visit. I could tell her anything. She never said a scolding word. Never tsked when I told her about a failed test or a situation with a boy or my friends. When Kurt Turner got me pregnant, Mama put her hand on my belly and spoke gibberish about the "angel within, waiting to get out." She never made much sense, but I liked that at least her attitude toward the babies—unlike everyone else I knew—was one of love. So when they were finally born, naming the girl Cassidy Penelope Turner felt natural; it was the name of someone who loved the idea of my babies, perhaps even more than I did.

When I got to the top of the steps and opened the door to Mama's bedroom, I hadn't expected that the smell of her remains could grow worse, but I was wrong. I held my nose as I opened the door. Clara had set both house fans around her, in a failed attempt to push the stale air around the room. She'd kept the shades drawn to keep out the sunlight heat, but now that the sun had set it had the opposite effect. Holding my breath, I lifted both shades, opened the windows wide and leaned out to breathe oxygen untainted with rot. Even the evening, with its cloud-streaked sky and dark abyss of the woodland acres, lent no release. I willed away my gag reflex, catching in the dark the form cloaked head to toe in a white sheet. The stuff of ghosts, I thought, imagining her soul, trapped by bedding, might rise and take form beneath them. But Mama would have never been that kind of ghost. I knew she believed in them, and in angels, too. Said she'd seen them, even talked to them, every so often.

I took out the watch stuffed in my jeans pocket and held it up to my ear. Maybe it did belong with her. I glanced toward the door. Mr. Burns would be up here any moment. But I wanted to see my mother, one last time, to tell my daughter about it, to remember all I could about her namesake. I turned on the light closest to the bed, a dingy 40-watt bulb that barely lit the room. I hovered over Mama's bed. Clara had left her in her nightclothes, said she didn't want to disturb Mama from her resting place. I'm sure it was because she couldn't handle the body well. Nylons catching dead toenails, seams ripping around an elbow that refused to bend. I could not blame her. The bedding seemed to be damp in places. I took hold of the sheet—which Aunt Sarah kept calling "the shroud"—and folded it back with all the ease of someone unaware of what awaited her.

My mother and Clara had once shared the same nose, but no longer. Her face had distended some from the heat and her entire form had bloated. Her wrist had swollen to twice its size and I knew I couldn't return the watch, even if I tried. The strap wouldn't reach.

Just then, the somber eyes of our ancestors in photographs in twinset oval frames came into view on the wall above my mother's head. Finally, the open window served its purpose, because I found myself hanging out of it, stomach empty save for the bile, and that's all that came up. I drowned out everything, eyes fixed on the darkness, until I heard Clara's voice mingling with my daughter's cries. I turned. It was Aunt Sarah, eyes ablaze.

"You ain't got no business in here," she said. "Get on out to your mongrel."

"You want to talk mongrel?" I asked. "Go watch your daughters eat the skin off chicken."

It's beside the point to say that she slapped my face for my sass, and called me a "no-good whore," no doubt waiting a long time for the chance to do both. And to my surprise, I slapped back. One solid slap echoing another, and the glower of red on my face held longer than it took for me to reach my room, where little Cassidy, hungry for her milk, fell silent in my presence. We sat together in the dark, rocking, her mouth on my breast, the whir of the tiny fan nearly drowning out the voices vibrating through the wall, the opening and closing of drawers and closets. As I clutched the dead watch in the dark, I imagined the undertaker's skin flaking on the bed sheets, while Clara and Aunt Helen and the others fussed over which dress, already in the mindset of who gets what. And yet here was Cassidy, each thump of her little heart coursing through my fingertips, each beat a reminder that we would, and must, move on.

THE DUCK WALK

I AM A KNOWN HERETIC IN THESE PARTS because I mow the lawn on Sundays. I can feel my neighbor's eyes on my back on the Lord's Day as I maneuver through my special, signature Square-in-a-Square mow pattern, or when I take out the trash, or clear brush from the swamp. I know they're watching, and so for the hell of it I'll sometimes go bare-chested, pot-belly-proud like my Daddy. If I think of it, I'll up the throttle on the mower right when the neighbors drive by. And I slow and scowl at them, and they slow and scowl at me, and it's like I'm telling them with my eyes: Mowing the lawn on Sundays is not a sin. And the look in their eyes says back: Yes, it is.

And today the child's eyes are on me, too. She's my sister Anna's kid, going on five. Cassidy Penelope. It's classic Anna to pick for her child the longest, most complex name she could find. Why not just Cass, like our Mama? It's also just like Anna to up and leave a situation that doesn't suit her, and then call one of us to go and comb it all out. Like leaving Cassidy Penelope on a friend's porch so she could go fight fires in Montana. Then calling our sister Clara from a bus stop in west Kansas to ask if the child could come and live with us instead.

You should have seen Clara when she got the call. She walked all the way from our house to the Gas 'N Sip, all ticked off in her housedress, looking like some sweat-hog's sister in orthopedic boots, with the curlers ripped from her bangs.

"Anna told me Cass is my second chance," Clara had said. "She said, 'You raised me; Look how well I turned out.' I could just kill her."

It is not easy being the brother of these women. Ma always liked to say before she died that each of our fathers was as different as they make men, and she had the kids to prove it. We each turned out favoring our daddies: Clara all stern and round; me, oil-stained hands, sandy-brown all over and sideburns to boot; Anna red-blonde and vixen-trim and always on the take. Ma's age caught up with her after she had Anna, but even before she died, she'd always kept to Clara to look after us.

And why Anna picked firefighting over child raising is beyond me. I know some women just aren't hardwired that way, and, to be sure, Anna got the calamity gene from her daddy. Even when she was a baby, she'd explode at the slightest sign of something gone wrong. I can remember when she was nine, her little lungs blew out the eardrum of a classmate who'd joked about our mother going bald. Later she and her best friend Dora would sneak out braless in suede skirts, taking backseat double dates with college boys. They'd give out names that matched their hair color, like Noir and Rouge. They'd come back late and fight on the front porch with Clara about sex laws and curfews. When Anna got pregnant—surprise, surprise—she'd use the phone and holler long-distance cuss words at her ex-boyfriend Kurt, who left for his station in Germany not long after they split.

It was no surprise that Cassidy Penelope and her twin brother were born with screaming in their cells. I drove Clara to see Cassidy Penelope and Clay at the preemie ward, a few days after they were born, and even then, Cass's mouth was all puckered, her fists clenched and moving like a little prizefighter under a cake tray. Clara claims Anna's anguish is what made them come one month early, and why Clay died two weeks later.

"Anger pipes through the umbilical cord. It shows in the milk," Clara had said as we walked back from the burial in our backfield, right next to Mama. "Some babies can't take it, Andy. That child was poisoned."

"Don't go looking to lay blame," I told her.

"SIDS, my foot. Poor lamb. He'll watch over us now."

Well, all I can say is, if Anna wants fires to fight, they got plenty here in Mewborn. Like that little time bomb impersonating a lemon on the porch. It's not enough to say she is a quiet child, because she's been here a week and hasn't talked yet. It's a strange kind of quiet, too. There's something in that cinch-sack expression of hers that tells you she's taking in your every move, stockpiling it, like a miser of information, or a little judge whose job it is to clutch an ugly stuffed duck. So it makes me wonder if she's noticed my square-in-a-square pattern, if it impresses her how I hit every corner at a right angle, how I overlap the path by three inches so when it's finished the grain of the grass holds a striped pattern.

But I don't see how she could miss any of my signature lawn moves because her eyes follow me with such precision, they look like they'll turn rectangular and at one point I turn off the mower to tell her so. She was supposed to be at church like the rest of Mewborn. I'd planned to mow the lawn in peace like I always do and for a few hours not have to think about Clara, the Gas 'N' Sip, the child, or her little puckered mouth. Clara had made a big deal this morning about getting Cassidy Penelope all ready for church. She'd found an old yellow apron dress from a closet somewhere, got her nails clipped, her face clean. Pigtails. Scrubbed sandals. All of it.

"Your big Red Banks Baptist debut," Clara kept saying. Cassidy Penelope did look like a real little mini-beauty-queen girl with all the flounces, the kind you'd actually take to church on a Sunday morning and expect everyone to fuss over afterwards. But when I reached out to scruff up her hair, I noticed how each strand looked like it was made of copper wire, like her Momma's, just dying to get out from under the rubber bands and be free.

"So why didn't you go to church, Baby Girl?" I asked her. "Don't you want to go learn how to be good? Good with God?" Cassidy Penelope did not respond. I think she could sense that even I did not believe what I was saying.

Even with the yellow dress and pigtails, even though Clara had given Cassidy Penelope her very own children's picture Bible, when we pulled up to Red Banks Baptist Church, the child refused to leave the car. She cinched up her mouth and shook her head from the back seat of the Crown Vic. Her arms and legs folded up onto themselves, trapping the stuffed duck in the knots of her body, like an angry pretzel in a yellow dress. The child would not go and Clara did not insist.

"I can't take a stubborn child to church," Clara said. "Not today. I'm on schedule to give the host."

"What about saving her lost soul?" I said, as Clara swung open the door and got out of the car, yanking the static from the ass-end of her dress. "Suffer the children?"

I told that child a whole string of knock-knock jokes all the way home and she didn't laugh at a single one. Wouldn't even say, "Who's there?"

So THERE THE CHILD SAT ON THE PORCH, watching me as I pushed the mower in my special, signature, square-in-a-square pattern. When I'm done with the squares, I backtrack over near the swamp, and mow that, too, which is about as unsatisfying as having a remainder at the end of a long division problem. I'm sure Cassidy Penelope noticed me mess up at one point. When I mowed the lawn, I wasn't used to an audience.

"Don't you want to color?" I said, in a lame effort to distract her. Cassidy Penelope held her stuffed duck even tighter to her chest and sat down on the porch steps. I gave up and started to mow again, thinking about how different Sundays were for me. Before she left,

Dora would come by in her red truck and after the lawn was done, we'd go into the house and get wild like we liked.

Ever since they were kids, Dora and Anna were always more like sisters in spirit than Clara could ever hope to be. And together they were about as dangerous a combination as bleach and ammonia. It was Dora who came up with the schemes they'd try to pull on Clara; it was Dora who'd introduced Anna to Kurt downtown; Dora who pushed me out to the back field one night, where her family's property meets ours, and with her blue eyes shining made me love her. She was seventeen then, I was twenty-two. The thing with Dora is her teeth are spaced out and strangely shaped, and yellowed from the liquid penicillin her Meemaw gave when she was a baby. Even then, when she smiled, you didn't really notice the gaps in her upper deck, the bicuspids below crammed above her jaw like shoppers at Christmas. She'd been taking a few classes out at Mewborn College after she got her GED, and she'd visit the station every day with some snack from her uncle's store, a Drake Cake or Lemon Fruit Pie or Hostess Honey Bun. Then there were our wild Sundays, and dinner out at Elm Center Café twice a month. Sometimes she'd stop in to visit with Anna and Cassidy Penelope, and stick around, waiting for Clara to go to bed so we could go to mine.

Until she got pregnant, life with Dora in it for those five years had been all right. And you'd think a baby might firm up the general plan of spending your life together with someone, and I believed until the moment Dora left me to go to Massachusetts that that was the case. But she came to see me with her car packed to tell me she'd gone to see the doctor, and, even though we'd told everyone to the contrary for the past two months, she was no longer pregnant.

"Tell them I lost it," she'd said. She was smoking a cigarette, leaning against her car in the dark. "Tell them it's none of their goddamn business."

My friends down at Duck's always ask what I'm going to do next, when I'll get out from under Clara's batwing. It's like they forget it's been years since Dora left and there's no one else around to take Clara to make groceries, to carry her to church, to the doctor's. And she won't get her license, even though I told her it's easier than a tractor, and faster, too. I've come close a few times to answering an ad for a vacant apartment in the paper, but I don't care to spend my money on couches and dishes and vacuums all that. And it's not like I enjoy washing my own clothes, or that I'm some primo chef or anything.

Still, where I live it is not easy to get laid, especially when Sunday morning is my main window of opportunity, since having your sister asleep in the next room while you're trying to get it on kind of defeats the purpose. I got a Maybe once from a gal up in Chicod said she might swing by sometime. And even if she never shows, there's always the lawn to mow. And there's the church-going neighbors to piss off, and there's my guitar, and beer, too, as long as I remember to buy it on Saturday. And now there's Anna's child to look after. But you can only do so much for a kid who doesn't talk, or cry, or tell you her ducky's name.

But I got to say, Cassidy Penelope won't stop watching me. I sneak looks back at her from time to time to see what she's up to. All she does is clutch her duck, and ignore all the crayons and the teakettle and the stuffed rabbit and Clara's *Redbook* magazine I'd set out special for her. So I figured maybe I ought to give her something to look at if that's all she's gonna do. So I start to skip and mow. I mow walking backwards. I duck-walk. And I don't look at her once. Because I know that's what she wants.

My silly moves make me think back to when we were kids, even before Anna was born. Clara would put a parlor doily on my head and make me wear one of Ma's old dresses. We'd drink sugar water from plastic teacups and play Visitor on the porch. Sometimes Ma would join us, her legs crossed in slacks, feet in slippers, and pretend to sip tea, too, joking how much I must like my big sister 'cause I let her put me in a dress. And I'd make them laugh, walking around the front yard on my tip-toes with a teacup in my hand, pinkie extended, eyes crossed. And you could catch Anna at any age lying there for hours drawing in her sketchpad, and later, smoking cigarettes in a mini skirt or a tie-dye sundress at sunset. Sometimes, Anna's daddy, before he left us for good, would get all generous with us and he'd bring home ice cream, and Ma would get out of bed for it and we'd eat it right there on the front porch to keep from Clara fussing at us about the mess in the kitchen. Those ice cream nights made you forget awhile the rotten-egg stench from the swamp, that Mama was sick, that Clara at sixteen was running the show. Anna rarely left Mama's side then. I guess she needed her more than any of us did. And now here Cassidy Penelope needs Anna. Or somebody.

At one point during my duck walk, I messed up the mow line. I gestured to the child in a theatric "can you believe this mess?" straight out of the Marx brothers. To my surprise, her knees were bent, her bottom extended, hands on her hips. Mimicking me. Looking like a duck herself. And it hit me that maybe Cassidy Penelope just needed someone who would play with her. She needed something fun like duck walks and maybe ice cream, so she'd know that the people in our family aren't a bunch of angry idiots who leave each other on people's porches. So I cut the engine again and called her to talk over the ice cream situation, and her scowl shifted to a grin after a minute as she kicked barefoot at the grass clippings.

"Wait. Does a grin mean, 'No, Uncle Andy, I don't want ice cream?'" She shook her head like it would fall off, still grinning. "I see," I said. "I figured a little girl looking as ducky as you might like ice cream."

Instead of returning to the porch, the child followed me as I pushed the mower. After a while, she skipped in big steps, holding her duck by its wing, trailing me as I completed my Square-in-a-Square mow pattern. She turned a few somersaults that stained her dress and showed her underwear. The grass covered her in clippings and I figured I'd let Clara deal with the stains, the blades of green trapped in her hair, stuck to her legs.

When we got to the swamp, I cut the engine and got on my haunches to tell the child a few things. First, to stay away from the stone wall. I told her to not even think about catching frogs, or going for a swim in the green gunk that some people around here call a pond because I wouldn't jump in and save her if she did.

And it took just a moment for me to turn my back and then, over
the growl of the engine, catch a whiff of her howling waist-high and
paralyzed in green water, her little legs trapped in the vines of lily
pads. Her whole body splashed down in the mess when she tried to
run. As I jumped in to untangle her, I could see the ruby pink swamp
flower she probably tried to pick and I held her to my chest. The lily
pads had trapped her good. I carried her to the grass and the green
clippings clung to us and I smoothed her hair and told her we'd be
okay. And she cried for a long time, these loud, messy sobs like I've
never before heard and all I could do for her was sit in the grass and
hold her to my chest and wait. Finally, she whimpered one little word
in a voice so quiet that I had to huddle close to her mouth to hear.

"What's that, Baby Girl?" I said.

"Holly," she said. She pointed to the swamp. The ducky. Fuck.

"I'll get her."

Probably the last place I'd want to be is on my knees, elbow-deep
in muck, looking for a goddamn ducky and instead pulling up an old
housedress. Or plastic baby bottles with ratty ribbons around them.
I found three pacifiers and tiny shoes and no duck anywhere. And I
think the other last place I'd want to be was on that lawn, dumping
before the child the mess of bottles and binkies and baby shoes and
handing her the pond flower and telling her I couldn't find Holly the
Duck.

I might have gone back to get it right then for the look on her face,
but I had my own grief to deal with, because I knew now what Clara
had done with the party favors she'd bought for Dora's baby shower.
Clara hated to give Anna a shower for the twins, said she didn't deserve
it, but Mama won out. She didn't think Dora deserved a shower either,
but since I was the father, Clara decided to go all out. She came out
of the Woolworth's one day loaded down with bags of pacifiers and
bottles and ribbon and such and spent the next three weeks filling the
bottles with lilac-colored M&M's, stitching up pale pink and blue bows
to tie around everything. I told her it was too early to think about a
shower, that Dora was hardly showing. But Clara jumped the gun as
only she knows how. She said there was a sale. She said she wanted to

be ready. And of course, thanks to Clara, the whole town knows how Dora went and saw the doctor before she left for Massachusetts.

Looking at the mess of it at my feet made me wonder what else Clara had dumped in that swamp, what I'd find if I went back in there. The child calmed a little when I told her I'd go back later for her duck with a fishing net. "If it's in there, we'll get it outta there," I said. "But not right now."

We were covered in the scum of the algae, the grass clippings, the swamp-bottom mud. But that was nothing compared to the smell of sulfur. I knew better than to even try to get into the house to wash up. I carried the child to the shed, found the garden hose, and took aim.

It probably wouldn't have mattered even if I had changed the setting to spray. The child screeched when the water caught her in a full-force jet-stream on her chest. She ran back to the front yard, toward the swamp, screaming as though I'd shot her with a BB gun. When I caught up to her, she already had in her grasp one of the muddy bottles. I grabbed her by her wrists and told her she had to stay away from that swamp. I sounded angrier than I really was, but she had to understand. She'd already nearly drowned. Her tears cleared paths down her dirty face as she collected the pacifiers, the little shoes, into the apron of her dress.

"I need you to say yes." I told her. "I need your word." She nodded but wouldn't look at me and I picked her up and carried her back to the shed, and it was then I decided I needed to fill up that sinkhole swamp for good.

I filled a bucket with water and tried to get her to wash up with me, at least our hands and faces, but she wouldn't. I even put the garden hose in her hands, showed her how it worked. Still, she wouldn't take aim at me, even though I deserved it. Instead, she started to sort into piles all the party favors: the filthy pacifiers and bottles, the pairs of baby shoes. Then she dipped each one into the bucket and set them to dry on the lawn. I tried to distract her with the idea of ice cream. I told her that we couldn't have ice cream unless we got clean cause they'd never let us in the shop elsewise. She did not seem to care. When I wiped muck off the face of my watch, I saw that we'd almost be late to pick up Clara if we didn't leave right then. I found a plastic tarp in the shed and spread it out across the front seat of the Crown Vic. The swamp gunk had begun to crust up our skin and clothes. I carried the child to the car, plopped her down on the plastic, and drove into town. Her dress looked gray nearly, and that little apron made a filthy nest for the pacifiers and bottles in her crisscrossed legs and the entire car smelled like eggs gone to shit. Even her pigtails looked like rattails now, all slick and stuck together in a half-dozen stiff points. I looked into the rearview mirror at my own muddy reflection and laughed aloud. We'd looked so regular and clean when we dropped off Clara. Now we had on us the mud and the swamp stench, the filthy clothes, all those binkies and bottles pulled up from the bottom of God knows where. I could see Clara lecturing us both the whole way home about the perils of the swamp, about Cassidy Penelope's ruined dress. And those shower favors, which, I might add, Clara had claimed she'd given to charity. I was so worked up about what Clara was going to say I almost didn't see Cassidy Penelope point at the sign for the Golden Goose Car Wash across the street from the church.

I guess maybe the goose logo reminded the child of her ducky. But I have no excuse for what I did next. I pulled in, fed the machine a few dollars, and hit the button for Basic Wash, and rolled down our windows. I put the Crown Vic in neutral and let the auto track guide us through the yellow cement bay. The child clutched one of the bottles to her chest like she had done with her ducky.

"You got to close your eyes, now. Hold your breath when I tell you," I said.

The green light flashed and the motors inside the car wash bay started rumbling as we moved ahead. The child closed her eyes and I closed mine as the first blast of warm water and suds shot into the car. I whooped when it hit, then laughed so she'd know it was all right.

When I said, "Now," I felt her little hand reach for my thumb on the steering wheel. She pulled my hand to her chest, and I was glad that our eyes were closed, glad that we'd be clean, or nearly so, for Clara when we picked her up. No doubt she'd be mad about the wet upholstered seats. But I'd coddle Clara with the promise of ice cream, lay out the tarp on the floor of the backseat to keep from wrecking her special ortho shoes. Besides, even if the backseat were damp, it wouldn't kill her if her ass got a little wet on the way home from church. Maybe it would help cool her off.

We'd figure it out later. It crossed my mind that the child might inhale a pile of suds, that I'd have to rewire my radio, that the floorboards of my car would probably rot from all the water. But I was just glad then for the soft blue and yellow brushes whipping the side of the car like the world's biggest set of feather boas. I was glad for the water and suds washing over me and the child, those boa licks on our arms, and I hoped the sorry, soapy mess of it all might take away more than the muck and stench of the family swamp.

SELVAGE

THE BACK WINDSHIELD OF THE ANCIENT CHARGER WOULD NOT BREAK under Cass's hammer, and all she wanted was to tear that thing apart. She wanted to make the world's hugest mess in the back seat of the car, cast dangerous bits of smashed glass across the gas station bay. All week, as she helped prepare her Uncle Andy's car at the Gas 'N' Sip for its Saturday night demolition derby destruction at the Mewborn High School football field, she thought about the damage she'd do to that windshield. She thought about it as she spray-painted the number "sixty-eight" in lime green on the Charger's doors and hood, then made jagged red and purple "Greased Lightning" style flames over the rusted fenders. She thought about it as she rode her bike to fetch spark plugs and a fan belt at the parts store, and later that week as she lined the Charger's steering wheel, ceiling, and dashboard with egg crate foam from the five and dime. She'd gouged out the headlights and tail lights early on, but Cass figured shattering that glass would feel about as good as busting through the frozen crust of ice puddles: a hollow blistered potato chip sensation for the whole body. Only bigger and louder and messier.

But here she was, hammer in hand, and the back windshield refused to grant Cass the effect moving metal should have on glass. She could not break the window. She knelt on the trunk of the Charger, and with both hands wrapped around the hammer, struck the window with every muscle in her body. She hopped off the car and stood on the bay floor in a baseball stance and swung the hammer like a bat. She picked a spot on the glass, spray-painted it with an orange star, and then hit hit hit the center until Joe Gomez, her uncle's shop assistant, poked his head out from under the Charger's hood to watch her.

"Isn't there, like, a law in physics?" Cass asked. She gave the windshield another good hit. The July heat made the hammer handle slippery in her hands. "You hit something, you break it?"

"There's all sorts of laws," said Joe. "Hey, how old are you, anyway?"

Cass adjusted the goggles suctioned around her sockets and tried again, answering Joe's question with a few more blows to the glass. She knew from her Uncle Andy that Joe was at least five years older than she was, so maybe nineteen, and he'd already dropped out of school to work on cars at the gas station.

"Some people aim high," Uncle Andy had said once about Joe. "Others aim right for where they are."

What bothered Cass about Joe was not his vocation, but how he asked all his questions: for example, how old are you, anyway? As though her age was a big deal. What did he care? Her last lob against the glass caused the hammer's head to slip clean off its handle. It skidded across the bay floor. Joe handed Cass a mallet. When the mallet failed—Cass could tell straight off it was far too rubbery to shatter glass—she found a wooden bat from the backseat of the Charger and let it rip. The back windshield remained intact. Then Uncle Andy came out of his office, hands on hips.

"Hey, Joe-Joe, what's all this standing-around business?" he said. "We got to get moving." Uncle Andy looked annoyed as he took the bat from Cass and with one blow put a spider web crack in the back windshield. Another blow put the hole right through. Before Cass could stop him, Uncle Andy did the same with each of the other windows, the sound of shatter ricocheting across the room. When he was done, he leaned the bat against the tire wall.

"There. That should get you started, Baby Girl," he said. Then he kissed Cass on the cheek, put his hand on her shoulder so she'd meet his eye. She knew she failed to hide her disappointment. "Look," he said. "The Chargers they made that year were built to last and no little girl with a baseball bat will change that."

The Charger had belonged to Uncle Andy's daddy before he died, and for the past thirty or so years everyone in town told Andy they thought he was crazy to let it sit outside to rot in the back lot of the old man's station. But Uncle Andy said that it was his gas station, and that the Charger was exactly where it belonged. Its main flaw, Uncle Andy had told Cass, was that it had a weak universal joint that needed a few strips of metal reinforcement just under the front end. Joe had welded those in place the first day Uncle Andy decided he was going to enter the derby. "Gotta put something into it to get something out of it," he said.

Uncle Andy picked up the bat and handed it to Cass. Then he checked Joe's progress under the hood, investigating the new, disc-shaped Magnum air filter perched atop the mechanical guts of the engine, the sets of spark plugs guaranteed to make sure the Charger would run. He shut the hood and looked proudly at Cass's paint job, which did little to hide how badly the metallic blue paint had dulled, how scarred red with rust its backend tire wells.

"You done all right, Cass," Uncle Andy said, walking the length of the Charger. "She's a real artist, Joe-Joe, ain't she?"

Joe nodded as he took a drag from his cigarette. Uncle Andy went into his office and returned with a little white cowboy hat, which he duct-taped to the raised ridge of the hood. Then he stuck a skein of red Christmas garland across the single-panel grille.

"What do you think?" Uncle Andy asked.

"Like Christmas," Joe said. "Or something."

"You sure you want to put this in a derby?" Cass asked. "Aunt Clara said her church would take it as a donation. Paint it up and sell it."

"Over my dead body is this thing going to a bunch of Free Will loonies," Uncle Andy said. "This sucker is destined for the dump. Speaking of loonies, your Aunt Clara called to see when you were coming home for lunch. That was an hour ago. My recommendation is you get yourself home. We'll finish up here."

"But what about the windshield?" Cass asked. "I have to…"

"We got to get this underway Baby Girl, and you got to eat," Uncle Andy said. "You don't want to tick off your aunt. Go on now."

CASS RODE HER BICYCLE BACK HOME, annoyed about the windshield, her uncle's take-over ways. But she was used to it by now. It was all or nothing with Uncle Andy, and for most of Cass's short life, Uncle Andy gave her all he had. Cass's mother, Anna, had left her with Uncle Andy and Aunt Clara when Cass was five, and their little house on Penny Hill had been home ever since. She'd hardly had time to set her bike down on front porch steps when Aunt Clara asked her to go upstairs and clear out some space in the hall closet.

"I got two more rubber tubs sorted down here, and there's got to be a spot up there for them somewhere," she said.

"Can't it wait?" Cass asked. "I got to get back to the shop."

"I need this done when I ask for it," Aunt Clara said. When her aunt spoke slowly, pronouncing each word as though she'd put a period between each one, Cass knew better than to fuss at her. Aunt Clara had grounded Cass for a lot less than backtalk, and Cass couldn't risk it today. Given her aunt's struggles with diabetes—her heavy limbs and circulation boots slowed her down—Cass usually didn't mind helping out, passing a vacuum or helping with the dishes. But it always seemed to Cass that her aunt's efforts to tidy the house were somewhat mislaid. Aunt Clara didn't clean as much as she reconfigured and shuffled. She packed and unpacked. She organized, then stowed. Sometimes she hid things. But she never, ever, threw anything away. Plastic baggies and cereal box liners were hand-washed and hung to dry on the line alongside underwear and T-shirts. When the T-shirts grew holey, they'd be clipped to dust rags. And when they were done being rags, Aunt Clara would tuck them into the spaces between the walls and floor to keep at bay cold weather and pests.

So it was no surprise when Cass found a pair of suitcases on the uppermost shelf in the upstairs closet stock-full and heavy. One nearly knocked her off the stepladder as it fell to the floor and snapped open. Out tumbled a suede miniskirt with industrial snaps up the front. A half-dozen cotton sundresses in faded floral patterns. Thin-skinned, hip-hugger bell bottoms worn in the thigh and seat. In the second suitcase Cass found scraps of fabric and dozens of patterns. Unused zippers, still stiff in the pack, and spools of thread. Yards of carefully folded fabric wrapped in plastic. Cass knelt in the hallway before the suitcases, surrounded by their contents. Aunt Clara came up the stairs with one of the tubs and found Cass holding to her chest a green dress.

"Your ma made that. Wasn't much she took when she left home," Aunt Clara said. She stepped over the piles and sat on the lid of the rubber tub. "She had a pack on her back and you in a stroller."

Cass pressed the dress to her face, taking in the smell of sandalwood and cedar. She knew her mother by this sylvan scent, had learned it during an outdoor concert. Cass was three, sitting on a square flannel sheet, watching her mother dance on the lawn to "Cinnamon Girl," her long red hair swaying, arms raised over her head like a wobbling set of antennae absorbing the energy from the music that swirled through the air in a thousand colors. At one point, she'd picked up Cass, swept her into that world of music and movement, and Cass held on, burrowing her head into her mother's neck, her little legs and arms wrapped around her mother's moving waist and shoulders, taking in the sandalwood. That moment had always stayed with her, even after her mother had gone to Montana to fight fires, and Cass had come to live with Uncle Andy and Aunt Clara.

"Not everyone's Mama can stick around to tend babies," Uncle Andy had told her, one time after her mother had come through town to visit, when Cass was seven. "That's why they make families, so we can all take care of each other."

Cass looked for tags on her mother's green dress and found none. She traced with her fingertips its inner seams, then its hemline, each stitch near perfect.

"Did she make these clothes by hand?" Cass asked.

"There should be a sewing machine up there," Aunt Clara said. She looked up into the closet and pointed at the baby blue Singer stowed in the back corner. "Yep. A present from her daddy. Mr. Breckenpaugh, wherever he is."

Cass tried to imagine her mother hunched over the Singer, assembling cut pieces of cloth secured by straight pins, driven by the up and down rhythm of the machine. Or whip-stitching the tethered thread for the hem, the needle sharp and pinched between her fingers. Cass had one small photograph of her mother that she kept in her room, a school portrait in black-and-white. She could just imagine her mother squinting with her wild hair in the sunlight of her yellow bedroom that now belonged to Cass, emerald fabric draped across her lap.

Cass took down the sewing machine and brought it to her room. Then she took an armload of her mother's clothes from the suitcase, the A-line skirts and paisley suitcoats and sundresses, and tried on each of them, stepping out into the hallway from time to time to show Aunt Clara, who was still rummaging through the closet. There was a pair of skin-tight, store-bought jeans that fit Cass perfectly. A halter-top made of neckties, all sewn together in a silken patchwork. She'd saved the emerald sundress for last, and when she tried it on, the twin French darts at the bust line barely accommodated Cass's small breasts. The zipper down the back had a good two-inch gap between the teeth. In the too-small dress, Cass found Aunt Clara in the hallway, sorting through the rubber tub of teacups wrapped in linens.

"I don't understand," Cass said. "Everything else fits."

Aunt Clara looked at Cass and the dress from over the tops of her glasses and turned her around.

"You know why, don't you?" Aunt Clara said. "She never bothered to wash the cloth. I told her to, but she was too gunned up to listen. Her first dress, and after one wash, it shrunk to nothing. Hardly fits a

Barbie doll. I went out the next day and bought her five more yards, washed and ironed 'em myself soon as I brought it home but she never touched it again. Typical Anna."

Before she went downstairs, Aunt Clara picked up a book from inside one of the suitcases and handed it to Cass: *The Reader's Digest Beginner's Guide to Sewing*. Aunt Clara said, "Looks like it could help you out, if you had an interest."

Cass looked through the book's instructions about seam lines and zippers, darts and patterns and measurements. She'd taken home economics that spring, had made a pair of pillows and a simple skirt with the sewing machine at school. Ten minutes later, she was still reading when the phone rang. She heard Aunt Clara call to her from the bottom of the stairs.

"Hey, Cassie! Thought you were in a hurry! Andy's on the phone, waitin' on you down at the station," she said. Cass put down the book and slipped on the jeans and the necktie halter-top, feeling a little older than her fourteen years. Then she went downstairs.

"Are you coming with us tonight?" Cass asked.

"Like putting lipstick on a corpse, those derby things are," Aunt Clara said. She handed Cass a paper bag filled with lunch. "It's ugly what they do. Killing cars. And they charge you five dollars to watch, too."

THE LAST CAR MOVING IS THE WINNER, Uncle Andy had told Cass before he pulled out of the pit area and onto Mewborn High School's football field. But what he must have failed to remember, as his wheels squealed beneath him and as he pushed peals of black smoke into the bleachers, is that even the best engine won't do you a lick of good if you don't have tires to take you there. Uncle Andy had Joe yank the back brakes from the Charger, and, as part of the uber-macho, pre-derby, rev-up psych-out session that featured the raggiest, nastiest auto swansong in four counties, Andy mashed his left foot solid on the brake as his right gunned the gas full-throttle. The Charger's back wheels spun and spun, tearing up the forty-yard line, and you could hear Andy whooping from inside the car. And the derby hadn't even yet started. A few people in the stands reported afterwards they'd timed a full minute of burning rubber revolution before the Charger's back tire blew. Maybe it was a pebble or some bit of glass or a bald patch worn thin. For a moment, the bang startled everyone in the stands who knew the real story about that Charger—had he blown out his brains like his own Daddy?—before Uncle Andy started to cackle again. He revved his car all the more. The white cowboy hat hood ornament turned gray with rubber dust.

"That goddamn Andy. All that screeching," Cass heard someone say in the stands. "And going absolutely nowhere."

Joe had gone home. He'd offered her a ride up to the derby in his brother-in-law's tow bed truck, which he'd borrowed to bring the Charger to the high school. But on the way there, he accidentally dropped the car off the bed's back end at the bottom of the Frog Level crossroads. Joe'd been the one who'd driven the Charger up the ramp and then left the car in neutral. Then he forgot to secure the emergency brake, used no chains to attach the thing, except for one long one in the front. And when the truck stopped fast, the Charger rolled back, and its ass-end fell clear off the flatbed. The bumper kissed the pavement, and nearly landed on Uncle Andy's trailing Crown Vic. Even Uncle Andy couldn't find anything to joke about as he got out of the car and found some chains in the trunk to help lower the other half of the Charger to the ground.

"Hell, Joe-Joe, you couldn't sell Band-Aids at a cat-fucking contest," Uncle Andy said. He downed some of his bourbon and tossed the chains to Joe. Together they extended the ramp and got the Charger back onto the tow bed. Cass watched them from the passenger seat of the cab. She'd been riding with Joe on his invitation, and just before he stopped fast, he'd asked Cass if she'd ever had a boyfriend, if she liked it when boys kissed her. He touched her shoulder and moved down to feel the strips of necktie that covered her chest, it was then that Cass screamed and pushed him away, and it was then that Joe nailed the brakes to keep from rolling through the intersection.

After the accident, Joe smoked in silence the whole way up to the high school, and Cass kept her arms folded tight across her chest, feeling like she should apologize, or change her clothes, even though she couldn't think of how any of what had happened was her fault. Was she sorry because she'd never kissed a boy? Sorry because she didn't think she wanted Joe to be the first one to do it? Sorry she'd made him brake too fast? As soon as the Charger was on the ground, engine running, Joe left Cass and Uncle Andy at the high school and did not say goodbye.

Now that the derby had started and Cass was alone in the stands, she wished Joe had stayed, at least for a little while. Even from the bleachers you could see Uncle Andy finishing the fifth of bourbon he'd started just before the derby. You could hear him hollering cusswords to his competitors as the emcee announced the names of all twenty drivers. Finally, the blowhorn sounded, and as the black dust from the tires and revving engines settled in a smelly tar haze, the Charger revved ahead. But the flat back tire kept the car from moving like its engine wanted and before Uncle Andy could get any traction, the first car hit the Charger perpendicular at a good fifteen miles an hour. Then the second car peeled out, donut style, a double-hit sidewinder that crushed Uncle Andy's driver's side door, then the front bumper. It was clear to Cass that her uncle's engine-revved preening had irked the other drivers, because each one had made it his business to seek out the Charger, to push and slam against it in a crushed metal crucifixion, like chickens honing in on and pecking away at the weakened leader of the flock.

It was not long after a swift head-on collision that the flames started under the hood and Uncle Andy hit his head, helmet and all, on the steering wheel.

"IT'S NOT LIKE THE GOAL IS TO RIDE THE CAR OFF THE LOT," Uncle Andy would say later, surrounded by medics, as he swilled a fresh beer, the helmet on his lap. "It's not like I didn't have fun out there, revving everyone up. And you, Cassie baby, running out there like Wonder Woman's kid sister or something. You coulda been killed."

Cass couldn't have felt more shamed. She'd seen the fire coming up from under the hood of the car, the red garland strewn across the grille smoking then turning orange with flame. She thought only of the killer engine, some thirty years old, the special spark plugs Joe had showed her, the rows of valves that reminded her of rib cages, the acid from the refurbished battery: all of it, melting into a fireball, contained under that hood and dripping hot onto some bit of oil or gasoline that would take away her uncle forever. He'd passed out from the head-on hit and no one but Cass had noticed. If she'd thought about it, she would have found a referee to sound the bullhorn. If she'd thought about it, she'd have never run into the middle of that torn-up football field with everyone she knew watching, all of them thinking, There's Crazy Andy passed out behind the wheel of his crazy dead father's car, and here comes his even-crazier niece trying to save him. It wasn't fair of Uncle Andy to laugh at her for running out amid the clashing metal cars—now that they were both safe and alive—for slipping into the passenger side of the car through the glassless window with the door welded shut to shake him awake and yell that his car was on fire. And only then did the bullhorn sound and the motors idle and the medics and the marshals come with badges and kits to put out the fire and carry Cass away. Her arm bled from a nub of glass left on the window. And she sobbed from the sidelines as the medics cut Andy free from the double-truck seatbelt and got him out through the driver's window. She heard someone call it extrication. And as her uncle came to, his confused slurs on the field turned to wildcat hooting, then anger, as he cussed out the men with extinguishers who snuffed the Charger's last chance of complete destruction. Then he cussed out the EMTs who'd gripped him by his arms, and the men were silent and dignified in their uniforms and they let Andy say what he needed to say about them and their goddamn mothers. And he wouldn't let the medics take him anywhere, said he was fine, and the destruction on the field continued until the driver of a copper-colored GTO emerged grinning from the driver's side window to collect the two-hundred-dollar prize.

*

WITH THE DERBY OVER, everyone had cleared out, and Cass and Uncle Andy sat on the uppermost row of the bleachers and watched the tractors and crushers that had been waiting dormant in the wings to take away the junked-up cars from the ruined football field. They were mechanical undertakers, men at work, serious and operating heavy equipment on overtime: an industrial plow, the powerful magnetic crane, that lifted each car as if by magic and transported it to the crusher that stacked and stomped the steel, clearing the field for the grounds crew the next morning.

"I bet all these boys who put this on make a right nice penny from it," said Uncle Andy.

"Where's the money in a bunch of junk?" Cass asked. "Isn't this just for fun?"

"Fun, yes, Baby Girl. But think about it. Everyone out there pays twenty-five bucks to be in the derby, right? And each person in the stands pays five. Best I can tell everyone in town but Joe-Joe and Clara came out for it," he said. "That's a lot of money, not counting all the behind-the-scenes wagers, which is where the real dough is."

The crusher started to make a loud pounding noise. Cass could see what was left of the Charger on top of the heap, the number "Sixty-eight" still visible between blows. She covered her ears.

"What gets me is these guys here are paying to haul all this away, too," Uncle Andy said, raising his voice. "The derby guys own the cars after we're done with them, and they get, what, fifty bucks a car, scrap metal. Amazing. All they paid was the seed and labor to fix the football field and that two-hundred-dollar kitty for the guy in that piece of shit GTO. Not bad for a night's work."

Cass thought of how wild Uncle Andy had been in the Charger, how different he seemed at the height of his liquored state, how he'd catcalled the contestants, spinning wheels until the tire blew, reveling in the destruction of a perfectly good vehicle. But she loved him most when he was quiet like this, when he just explained how things were. Last year, he'd brought her up to the roof to fix the TV antenna and they stayed there looking for satellites in the night sky amid the pulsing glow of the power lines, and he'd told her about the stars and how television worked. His voice now was soft, like it was on their dark roof, and Cass had no doubt that she mattered to him, that he loved her.

"Why did you get so crazy out there?" Cass said. "You could have won the whole thing. That Charger was as good as new."

Uncle Andy looked away for a minute, felt in his breast pocket for his cigarette pack, which wasn't there. He took both of Cass's hands instead.

"My daddy left me that car when he died," Uncle Andy said. "And he didn't just keel over like a normal person, or die in his sleep at home like your Meemaw. Now, Aunt Clara don't want you to know this, but she's not here to stop the telling. You know that gas station was his. Going there every day reminds me of him, how I found him dead in the back bay, still holding his revolver. And in his goodbye note, that bastard left me the car, said he'd washed and shined it especially for me. That I could finally drive it now that he was gone. All I got to say is if he wanted to do me any favors, he could have just stayed alive and given me the car. Or at least let me drive it sometime. Or hell, he could have driven his sorry ass out west with it to live out his days. He never got over your Meemaw, even though it had been a good ten years since she left him for your granddaddy. I couldn't hear enough from people telling me what I should do with the car: did I want to sell it, store it, donate it. Hell, if I'd kept that Charger indoors it would have been a classic. You could have driven it in a couple years, been the talk of the town, Baby Girl. That top-of-the-line Charger, all mine, rotting in the back lot."

Cass shivered a little; it had turned cool and her necktie halter-top didn't cover much of her back or shoulders.

"Did you know my momma used to sew her own clothes?" Cass asked.

"Yeah, Clara told me on the phone today you'd found the sewing machine and all that stuff your momma left in her suitcases. Clara was so funny, she said, 'Looks like we got Anna living upstairs all over again.' You look just like your momma, you know. Same wild hair, for sure. Boys better watch out for you."

The crusher stacked and stomped the last of the ruined cars. It was getting late and Uncle Andy said he had plans to meet his buddies down at Duck's Tavern.

"Funny thing what we do with the gifts we're given," Uncle Andy said. "Don't let me be your guide on this one, Baby Girl. You did a good thing saving me from the wreck and all. But don't take any lesson from what I did tonight."

UNCLE ANDY DROVE CASS BACK HOME. Aunt Clara was sleeping when she came in. When she turned on the hall light, Cass noticed that her new jeans were stained with blood. Her whole body was dusty from dirt and burning rubber. She went upstairs to find the mess of her mother's clothing on the floor. The patterns that made her mother's A-line skirts and drop-waist dresses and button-down blouses were scattered in their packs. Cass opened a few of the pattern packs to find them trimmed and folded with precision. It was impossible to refold them as they had been, impossible to remember which thin sheet went with which pattern, and to return them to their proper envelopes. The thin paper crinkled and threatened to tear with every fold. She could not find the pattern for the green dress. That first, perfect dress made in haste. She could see her mother throwing away the pattern, too wounded by the rookie move she'd made forgetting to wash the cloth. Or maybe she'd just had an idea in her head for the sundress: it was all before her, the tight bodice, the two-inch straps, the A-shaped skirt, no pleats, the hidden zipper. Maybe no pattern for this dress had ever existed.

Among the packages Cass found just one unopened pattern for a little boy's sailor-style jumpsuit. She opened it and unfolded the rectangular onionskin sheets, and laid them out on the floor. She found the green dress from the pile of loosened patterns and held it up again to her body as she consulted the Reader's Digest sewing guide, then used the tape measure to find the size of her waist, her hips, her bustline.

She laid out her mother's dress over the sheet, as the guide suggested, and adhered to the seam lines as she drew each piece of the dress over the old jumper pattern, careful to make her outline a good three inches larger than the dress itself. She used a soft carpenter's pencil, then a black Sharpie marker, and did not tear the paper. As she traced the bodice and skirt panels, she wondered about the factory-design outline for the tiny jumper pieces, the sailor hat and collar shirt. She thought of Uncle Andy, in those last moments of spinning wheels, his cheeks red from smiling and from bourbon, before the great pre-derby tire pop, the double-sideline hit that knocked him out, the hood fire that took him out of the running. Who in those stands but Cass would have ever looked closely enough inside the Charger to know Uncle Andy had passed out, to see that his father's old car was on fire, to go out there and make sure he'd get out alive?

Cass went downstairs in the dark and found the scissors and iron in the kitchen. Uncle Andy would be out at Duck's for a few hours yet, looking for Joe, no doubt retelling his stories until his pals told him to shut up already about his screech-wheel flat tire, the smoky haze ricochet ride on the football field. How Joe had let the Charger fall off the tow bed, how his niece cut her arm and nearly broke her neck getting him out of the flaming car. And Uncle Andy would cast himself as the star of his very own mini-drama, and unless you were there in the bleachers and saw it with your own eyes, you'd have never guessed he was the first one knocked out of the derby. He'd be in the tavern, all revved up with liquor like he liked, imagining he could cruise forever through Mewborn's bars on the shelf life of his tall tales.

Cass returned to her room and cut along her magic marker guide, careful to replicate the line of her mother's design. The green fabric looked vast to her when she laid it out on the hardwood floor. Five yards. Fifteen feet. Even as she pinned the pattern pieces to the fabric, and began to cut, and later sew, it felt impossible that she'd be able to create something to wear in the world made of her own hand.

PROOF OF ME

Cass moved to San Francisco for Dave, and she stayed because of Amar, who used to go out with Jonah. Except for Gwen, who found a houseboat to rent, they all lived together with Jeremy and Aaron in a fourth-floor apartment on a side street just past Japantown.

Amar was a sculptor of hungry ghosts and Cass loved her from the start. They'd spent nearly every night together that spring, away from their exes, roof-camping in a blue dome tent. They woke early, even though their schedules did not demand it: Cass handed out leaflets for peepshows and timeshares. Amar made clay vessels in her studio. One day, without asking, she cut off Cass's ponytail.

It was cold that morning, and Cass was looking out the window of the courtyard apartment, huddled in a silky sleeping bag when she felt the cool scissors slip across the nape of her neck. The children on the third-floor were eating dry cereal in bed. A waist-naked couple argued as they clutched coffee cups to their barrel chests. The first-floor tattoo artist, exquisite with her pigment, stuck her needle into an early morning customer. Amar gave the scissors a squeeze. The tip of the blade caught the sleeping bag and its downy stuff billowed in puffs as the amber ponytail fell to the floor. Cass shrieked as though each cut strand was connected to a nerve somewhere inside her. When she stammered "Why?" and touched her head to feel what remained, Amar held out a vessel.

"You're just not imagining the possibilities," Amar said. "Your hair will do society far more good as artwork than it ever will on your head."

Amar's vessel had a thin vein of black that cut through the coppery glaze like frozen thread. It came from a hair, she said, that she'd found in a fresh pack of clay.

"Don't you think it's beautiful how something so random like a strand of hair can change everything?" Amar said. "Whose hair is this? Whose DNA?"

Cass looked at her reflection in the window, her hair now just reaching to her earlobes in an unsteady line, her expression a scowl. She grabbed the scissors from Amar and cut the rest of her wiry red hair as short as she could, using the reflection in the window as her guide.

"Did you know that some painters will only use brushes made from the hair of professional Japanese sea-swimmers?" Amar asked, as Cass continued to cut. She went to the kitchen to check the tea on the stovetop, and returned with a plastic bag and broom to sweep up Cass's loose strands. Then she sat on the floor and held the secure end of her ponytail between the soles of her bare feet and began to braid it.

"Do the swimmers sell their hair, or does someone just come along and cut it off their heads?" Cass asked. She threw the scissors onto the floor. Amar unbraided the lock and walked to the mirror, holding Cass's hair like bangs across her own black locks, and then her upper lip. She parted it so two hanks hung down each cheek.

"Cassie, my love? There's a new sheriff in town," Amar said to the mirror, imitating Cass's North Carolina twang. The timer went off in the kitchen. Cass found her Sharpie marker began to draw a small bird on her inner wrist.

"Tea's ready," Amar said.

LATER THAT WEEK, Amar took Jeremy's crescent moon nail clippings from the coffee table and embedded them on a cup's lip. When Gwen emerged from her houseboat cloister to have dinner with Amar and Cass, Amar collected a jar of her spit to fold into clay. In two weeks, the living room was filled with vessels that contained the DNA of nearly everyone Amar knew in San Francisco, but she wouldn't say whose vessel was whose.

"If it's part of you, you should know when you see it," she said. "Like those reincarnated lamas in Tibet. They always know to pick which spoon was theirs."

EVER SINCE SHE MOVED TO THE APARTMENT, Cass spent her mornings watching the tattoo artist work. Growing up in North Carolina, she'd always thought of tattoo parlors as part of some nighttime endeavor involving the unfortunate convergence of hard liquor, a sharp needle, and the Tasmanian Devil forever on your back. Cass liked that this woman worked mornings. She longed to be under her needle, to submit to the pain required of an eternal mark. She wanted to sit in the artist's modified barber's chair, endorphins racing, and breathe the burning hot scent of her scarred skin as it filled with color, cerulean and magenta. She'd tell the tattooist, I know you. I know your work. She'd point to her window and say, I watch you from up there every morning. And from that day on, the tattooist would look over her shoulder, up toward the fourth floor, to see whether Cass was looking back.

But this scenario would never play out. Not because of money, but rather because Cass couldn't imagine what forever on her body was supposed to look like. But she'd consider the question daily as she handed out leaflets for the peepshow. She'd continually poll her friends.

"A fish? You'll always be Pisces," Jonah had said. He'd joined her that day on her leafleting rounds. Offering paper to strangers.

"No fish," she'd said. "Isn't a tattoo just shorthand to tell people who you think you are? I knew a guy with a cornucopia on his shoulder blade. Said it represented his offering to the world."

"Look at what you're wearing," Jonah said.

"He called it his 'bounty,'" Cass said. "What the hell is a bounty?"

"Seriously. How do combat boots and jeans cutoffs not contrive to say something about you?" Jonah said. "We're all in costume. Every piece of clothing makes a statement."

Cass tugged at her plaid button-down shirt, which she wore over a plain tank top. She'd worn the same pair of boots since high school. "Fine. I'll go barefoot. I'll go naked."

"You'd get no complaints from me," he said. "But you'd still be making a statement."

"So what can you be if you don't want to be anything?"

"You can be you," he said.

"How can you represent that forever? In ink?"

"Maybe start with what represents you now," Jonah said. "And go from there."

That evening, Cass began to draw tattoo contenders in her plain-paper notebook, and after a week went straight to her body. She'd use a Sharpie marker to draw symmetrical, looping patterns below her navel. A daisy chain down her arm. A sprawling cat on her calf. Once she wrote across her clavicle, "Make no stray marks." Once she drew a pencil thin moustache on her upper lip. She grew tired of each design just as the natural cycle of showers and the slough of skin made them disappear. "Who needs museums when we've got Cass?" Amar would say each morning between sips of chai.

THE DAY SHE MET JOIA, Cass had drawn a honeybee on her arm, just below her shoulder. Cass and Jonah were near the shore, handing out leaflets, when Joia walked up to Cass and cupped her hands around her bicep. She looked at her full in the face before she breathed in her ear: "Don't panic. There's a bee on your arm." Cass smiled, trying to calm the effect of the woman's hand on her skin, and told her to look again. Joia giggled into Cass's shoulder, her long hair whipping her face. She touched the bee with her pinkie.

"I know, silly," Joia said. "I just love tattoos."

"It's not a real tattoo," Cass said. "I drew it myself."

"Well, it looks like a real, live, fake bee tattoo," Joia said. "That's something."

Jonah walked over, handed Joia a leaflet, and invited her to their weekly potluck. Cass sat down on a bench to write out directions for Joia on the back of the leaflet. As she handed Joia the paper, the wind surged and took the stack to the sky. A hundred or more pages scattered across the beach and landed in the ocean, on the sidewalk, pink sheets pushed across the blue horizon. It was a beautiful waste.

JOIA ARRIVED TO THE HOUSE THAT EVENING LOOKING POSITIVELY Cleopatran. Everything on her draped and clung to her body. She wore bangles above her elbow and a tiara in her dark pageboy. Her smile had a triangular quality to it that suggested triangles were emerging from her hair, her shoulder shape, and the insteps of her bare feet, once she removed her gold spangled sandals. Cass regretted she hadn't changed from her cutoff overalls and sweaty plaid shirt. Joia had made a salad, deep green leaves from the farmer's market tossed in a wooden bowl. At dinner the hairs on Cass's arm stood at attention as Joia reenacted, with her mouth full of food, how she was tricked by the bee on Cass's arm.

"I thought it was a professional tattoo," Joia said. "You have an artist in your midst, I tell you." She surveyed Cass's cropped copper hair, her natural scowl, the locks whose tips she'd dyed bright red. "Look at those spikes. Like a woman on fire."

It was then that Amar began to tell Joia about her vessel project, her fascination with DNA infusion, the long dark strand of hair that had changed forever the possibility of her art. How she'd collected the DNA from her housemates and friends.

"You should have an exhibit, an opening here," Joia said. "It's a perfect space for it. Just like a gallery."

Cass found herself caught up in Amar's description of her work. She liked how vintage-sweet she looked in cat-eye frames and a green sundress of Cass's that no longer fit, her black hair swept into a ponytail. Cass looked at the vessels Amar had made, certain at least a few contained her hair. The vessels were impossibly tall and they took up most of the space in the living room. Amar had coaxed smooth planes of clay into oblong bowls, made warped spheres from mesh, shallow basins, frozen goblins. They had thin necks and huge belly-bases. Dave brought out his guitar after dinner and Amar and Joia walked around the living room, pretty visions dressed in jade and plum, talking about each piece as the others cleared the table. Then Cass heard Amar say to Joia exactly what she'd said to Cass when they first met.

Containment, Amar had told Cass, and now Joia, is what gives space meaning.

"You can put in anything you want." She cupped Cass's hands, then her own, in example. "Look. You could piss in it. Make a shrine. Hold a baby."

That night in the blue dome tent, Amar and Cass made love, sharing sweat and spit and fingertips all sticky warm, and Cass was grateful for Amar's touch even though Joia was on her mind. The next morning, Cass was downstairs at her window, watching the tattooist etch flames around a woman's navel, when Dave's door opened. Joia placed a single finger to her lips and smiled. As she passed Cass, the knot on her sarong slipped and she bent, bottomless and tanned, to collect it. She glanced back at Cass in a way that suggested she had perhaps let it fall for her benefit.

"I think Joia stayed with Dave," Cass told Amar when she arrived later with tea.

"I know," Amar said. "I joined them after you fell asleep. She's amazing."

Instead of responding, Cass focused on the tattooist below, trying to remove from her mind the combinations of Dave with Joia, Joia with Amar, Amar with Dave. She finished her chai quickly, swallowing the silty granules at the bottom of the cup. She returned to her blue dome tent and stayed there for the rest of the day, breathing deeply, telling herself it was important to remember that she had no claim on any other person.

Joia came to dinner that night, and stayed with Dave the rest of the week. Amar kept joining them after Cass had fallen asleep. But one night, and then the next, Amar didn't return to the blue dome tent at all. Then she didn't even stay at the apartment. Cass asked her about it after a week had passed.

"It's the tent," Amar said. "It smells too much of you. I'm sorry. I don't know how else to say it." Cass spent half a day's pay washing out her mortification at the Laundromat, airing out the tent, smelling everything for signs of her own scent. She'd stitched the gash in the sleeping bag where Amar had cut. Still, Amar never returned to the blue dome tent. When she was not downstairs, she stayed at Joia's.

When Joia came over, Cass took her meals on the roof, and at night she'd snake an extension cord for her lamp and alarm clock. She'd draw in the blue dome tent, as she listened to Amar and Joia make plans for the art opening. Dave and Jeremy played their guitars through the open windows. She'd listen and draw until she was too tired to do much else but fall asleep.

On the afternoon of her opening, Amar asked Cass go to the art institute neighborhood to hand out fliers to "people leaving the better art galleries." But most of the people Cass had come across were panhandling for change, not looking at art. Cass didn't want to invite any of these people into her home, art opening or not. She threw the invitations in the trash. She wanted to go to her tent, but knew if she returned too early, she'd have to shell peanuts for pad Thai or frost a cake for the reception. For weeks Amar and Joia were full-throttle planning for the opening. The apartment was filled with all of Amar's artwork, each object transported up four flights. Joia helped her to select and arrange the best pieces for the exhibit. They'd reconfigured the living room, took measurements to accommodate each piece, moved the sofa to the dining area, spent nights labeling postcards. They wrote to the local weekly arts papers, and the papers actually ran photos of Amar's work. When she saw the news clipping on the refrigerator, Cass knew they didn't need her stupid fliers to make the reception a success.

That afternoon, Cass went to the library and read through the classifieds in *The Examiner*, thinking maybe she wouldn't ever have to go back to her apartment if she came across the right ad. Where do you go, she thought, if you don't want to be anywhere? There was so much possibility in each typed classified line: Dancing Shoes for Sale. Treadmill, never used. Escort Wanted. But was it a car, or a woman? Or man? Cass wondered. She found a large atlas and studied the shapes of land, the stretches of blue pocked with pink little islands, the strange names of nations just north of the Lowlands, south of the Arctic Circle, just next to Russia: Svalbard. Jan Mayen.

She looked through every page of the atlas, taking in the topography, the capitols, the major cities and their insets, the landmarks and street names. She found North Carolina, and Mewborn, but not Penny Hill. She found California, eventually, and an inset of San Francisco. She located Japantown and traced Fillmore all the way to the public library where she sat, startled that she was somehow, however remotely, represented in the book. She contemplated the pink rectangle until the library lights flickered in signal of closing. When the wall clock struck nine, Cass realized she was late for Amar's opening.

The apartment was crowded when Cass got home. Nearly everyone was wearing pince nez-style masquerade masks with colored feathers across the brow. The vessels were aligned on the floor like pupils at desks, in columns and rows, a great physical matrix of all the people who had given Amar a piece of themselves. Cass found a little stool, her usual perch near the window, and had a seat.

Amar had been making each of her friends come before the crowd and guess which piece was theirs. She'd called on Jonah to select one of his. After he chose one correctly, Amar placed his name on three of them. She'd done the same with Dave and Gwen, Joia and Jeremy. Cass had found some carrots and hummus to eat as Amar said her thank yous to everyone, and she took in the scene behind her by looking at the reflection in the window.

"Thanks for showing up," Cass heard. Cass could see Amar behind a feather mask in the reflection. In one hand she held a drink, in the other was the mask's delicate stick.

"I'm sorry," Cass said. "I got caught up at the library…"

"I don't care about the library," Amar said. She set down the mask. "I called your name first tonight, out of everyone. I told them how you'd sacrificed your hair for art, for me, for my vision of you, and you weren't even here. How do you think that made me look?"

Amar walked to one of the vessels and picked it up and talked to it like it was a baby. Then she began to toss it lightly, from one hand to the other.

"Amar, would you put that down, please?" Cass asked. "You'll break it."

"No, Cass, I'll break you," Amar said. She stared at the pot as she spoke.

"That is not me," Cass said.

"What's you, then? You spend the day killing trees for peep shows, scribbling all over yourself, thinking you're going to get to the meaning of life from some stupid drawing of a duck on your ass," Amar said. "And here, you deny something that actually contains a piece of you?"

Amar tilted the mouth of the vessel toward Cass, in a way that suggested that whatever she'd say, the vessel would absorb it. But Cass didn't say anything. Before Amar went upstairs to the roof with Joia, she threw the vessel at Cass, underhanded, like a softball. Cass barely caught it.

"I am not your creation," Cass said loudly. The remaining guests held their masks to their faces as they looked at her, and Cass imagined each mask was a camera lens staring her down, taking in her greasy chopped hair, the faded Sharpie marker-design on her forearms, her unwashed, supposedly unfit-for-peepshows body. Cass fled the party, stomping downstairs in her heavy boots, and sat on the stoop of the apartment. She rummaged through her backpack and found one of the leaflets and realized the peepshow itself was probably open. She'd applied to work there when she first got to San Francisco, but the manager told her that she'd need to get her own costume, and even then, she was "probably not peepshow material." He told this to her halfway through her audition. He must have felt sorry for her because, even as she picked up her bra from the floor and slipped into her cutoffs, he told her he could set her up as a "promotional assistant" and have her distribute leaflets instead.

Cass was glad the manager who'd hired her wasn't at PixiDust when she got there. She found a vacant darkened closet and poured quarters into a slot to watch behind the plexiglass window a brightly-lit room full of bored women in fishnet tights and crotchless panties who opened and closed their legs for the other patrons. One turned cartwheels in high heels. Another gyrated her hips, making the little spangles jingle and move on her translucent skirt.

Cass would not have survived long in that bright box. She was much better with leaflets. Out of habit, she started to draw a few lines on her forearm with her Sharpie, not sure yet what she wanted to draw. She tapped at the plexiglass and asked one of the women through the voice box if she could have any tattoo, what would it be. The woman smiled at Cass and pushed her rear against the window. On the woman's left cheek Cass saw a pair of red lips and the words "Kiss This" in black cursive lettering. The shade lowered as Cass's time ran out, and she got up and left.

No one was up when Cass returned to the apartment. She did not go to her blue dome tent. Instead, she wrapped herself in a blanket and sat by the open window. In the dark she could make out the shape of Jonah's bicycle hanging on a cord from the ceiling and thought back to the first time she rode it across the Golden Gate Bridge, convinced the wind was going to blow her into the bay. Maybe she'd ride it home now to see her Uncle Andy and Aunt Clara. She'd cross the desert at night, her path marked by sand and snake on either side, a lone Joad in reverse, heading back East.

It was just light out when the golden spotlight of the tattoo artist's studio came on. Cass woke up sore from sleeping upright. She knew then she'd never get a tattoo, never sit in that woman's parlor chair. She wondered whether the money she'd saved for her tattoo would pay for a ticket to Svalbard. Perth. Mauritania. Cass crawled over to Amar's exhibit, each vessel still in perfect formation, a vigil sustained, unable to disperse. Assembled as such, and with nothing but the dark, quiet space around them, the vessels looked eerie, a few with long necks like some inhuman orifice, stretched mouths, forever open and imperfect. Odd bodies, naked and waist-high, aligned for inspection. Some of the porcelain basins were so shallow they could hardly hold water.

She rearranged the name cards Amar had placed in front of each vessel. Gwen Mavis I became Aaron Charles II. Aaron Charles I was Jonah Antrim III. Joia Loo moved to David Quentin. She found one of hers, Cassidy Penelope I, and kneeled before it for a moment before she picked it up and brought it to the open window.

Before she released it, Cass pressed her palms over the glazed grit. The wispy veins of her hair carbonized into a webbed pattern across the vessel, like a cave painting, the physical result of the spontaneous and the deliberate. She spit into it so it would not go down empty, and it slid through the tips of her fingers and plummeted to the courtyard below. The tattooist turned her head toward the window as the sounds of something breaking ricocheted against the walls. She looked skyward for the source, and gave a slow, uncertain wave when she spotted Cass.

Cass waved back before she returned to the exhibit, taking in the woman's bullring, her close-cropped crew cut and dark brown eyes. She found in Amar's formation another vessel that contained her hair, a tall one, unglazed, like a thin-necked bird's nest. She let that drop, too, and, after it landed, tried to find a pattern in the bone-white bits that had scattered across the cement courtyard. But there was none. Cass imagined at the next rain the little shards of clay and charred hair would find a home in the garden soil and begonias below and almost felt sorry she'd not be around to see it happen.

GESTATE

Cass stood in her kitchen, spooning vinegar into a bowl of mayonnaise, taking care it did not curdle. When it was ready, she added a dash of salt and dumped it on her boyfriend's head. Carlos eased back toward the sink to let Cass rub the mix into his scalp with her gloved hands.

It had been two months, and the lice had not yet left. Neither had Carlos, but that wasn't his fault. They'd agreed Carlos would move out as soon as he found work. And then the lice arrived. This was the fourth time Cass had fumigated the house and washed the sheets, clothing, and curtains. And earlier applications of blue, burning chemicals to Carlos' scalp had done little to kill off the parasites and their spawn. Cass had faith the mayonnaise would work.

Between the coin-op Laundromat and the infestation section of the pharmacy, Cass had spent a paycheck on lice removal products. Never had she bought so many shower caps. Rubber gloves. Detergent. Tiny steel combs. She'd come home that afternoon, late from an extra shift at the coffee shop to learn that, somehow, between watching sitcoms and cooking dinner, Carlos had caught lice again.

"This mayonnaise business sure beats chemicals," Carlos said. He tilted his neck to meet the pressure of Cass's gloved fingers, and his cheek brushed against her breast. "Maybe I should try to catch lice again."

Cass edged away.

"Sorry," he said.

"Let's hope this is the end of it," she said.

Cass wound a sheet of plastic wrap around his head, pressing it against his slick hair. She daubed a dry cloth around his brow and temple to keep the mixture from dripping into his eyes, and then covered his scalp with a shower cap.

"It says to wait an hour, okay?" Cass said, checking the directions in her library copy of Yen for the Moon: Managing Menses and Home Health. "Then we comb it out."

CASS SCANNED CARLOS' NECKLINE WITH A MAGNIFYING GLASS.

"They're everywhere," she said. "But at least they look dead."

Cass set down the glass and wrapped a large towel around Carlos' shoulders. She combed through his slick hair and sectioned his locks with a new rattail comb and plastic clips. She hunched under a bright reading lamp, careful to remove every egg, each dead body, with the steel comb. She wanted him clean. The sooner the better. Five days? Eight? The lice gestation period was relatively predictable. She'd give it a week. With every few strokes of the comb, she'd wipe its wire teeth with a tissue. As she completed each section, she contemplated how to tell Carlos, job or no job, he'd have to leave after this last round of lice were gone.

Tell him, she thought, combing just above his ear. Tell him you're through paying his way. Tired of coming home to jarred pasta sauce and the television and an unvacuumed living room. She hit a snarl at the temple and pushed through it roughly.

"How's it going up there?" Carlos asked.

"Almost done."

As she combed, she noticed the smallest of bald spots on the very top of his head. In their three years together, she hadn't seen it before. His hair was thick, with dark waves, and they'd joked that Cass, with her wispy copper locks, would probably go bald before he did. She touched the spot with her pinky finger and opened her mouth to speak, but Carlos began talking first.

"I've been thinking when this lice business is over, I'm going to move."

Cass stopped combing. "What about work? Where do you plan to go?"

"Anywhere. My parents, if I have to. I'll sleep on their couch in a shower cap."

Cass drew a deep breath. Carlos had been holding out to find a good job, not just any job; the lice had quarantined him. But in the past month, he'd stopped scanning the classifieds and instead sat watching TV, a notebook or his laptop across his knees, trying to make use of his time by writing a screenplay.

A screenplay!

When Carlos turned to face Cass, she took a step back.

"Watch your hair," she said. How could he not want to stay here until he found work? The apartment would be nearly empty without Carlos: the couch was his, the TV, too. No. This is good, she thought. He needs to leave. I don't even watch TV.

"I can't keep living off you," he said. "I don't know why I didn't move out right away, when we first talked about it."

Cass's laugh came out like a hiccup. "I know. The job…"

Carlos stared at his slippers, then looked up at Cass.

"It's not just about the job," he said. "I was ready to leave. But I'm still here. I thought maybe there was something making me stay."

"Are you talking about the lice?"

"Maybe, at first? I don't know," he said. "But all you want is for me to leave. I can tell."

Cass stared at the globs of oil trapped on the silver comb.

"That's not true," she said. "I don't think you should move to your parents."

"Where I go isn't your concern," he said. "Or, it shouldn't be."

Cass shook her head. "Can we talk about this later? When the lice are gone?"

Carlos arranged the greasy towel into a turban.

"Sure. But I'm moving on this," he said. "I'll call my folks tomorrow."

Cass didn't answer him.

"Are we done here?" Carlos asked, standing up.

"For now," she said. "Go shower. I have to check your scalp when your hair is dry."

Carlos closed the bathroom door behind him and Cass sat down at the kitchen table. She wiped back tears. She picked up the magnifying glass and stared at the last batch of nits trapped in the teeth of the metal comb. Dozens of sturdy, oval eggs trapped in oil, so many little lives. The vinegar loosens the eggs from the hair, she'd read; it doesn't kill them. Squished into tissues were the nymphs and adults, suffocated by mayonnaise oil, lanky with long front legs, each one shaped like a pale, flat ant. Five days from egg to nymph, she'd read. Three more to adulthood, then baby bites on the scalp. More eggs borne of human blood. Then what?

Cass looked at their apartment stripped bare of its linens. The wooden floor held the scuff marks of so many parties. They'd made love on the very chair on which she sat. She heard the familiar rumble of pipes and valves coming from the walls of the bathroom, and she squinted again at the eggs.

She raised the comb to her head and placed its tiny teeth against her scalp, closest to the part, and pulled it through her hair.

VACUUM

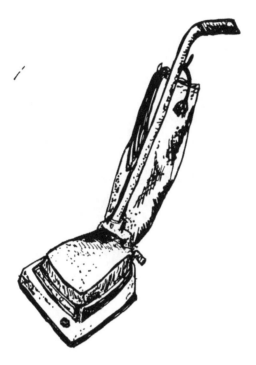

"Close supervision is necessary when any appliance is used by or near children. Do not allow vacuum cleaner to be used as a toy or to run unattended at any time."

Hoover Convertible Cleaner Owner's Manual

DISTANCE

THE ONLY WAY TO KILL THE FLEAS, Mama said, is to pinch them between your fingers and drown them in soapy water.

"If it's just plain tap, Shirl, they swim to the rim and escape," she said. "If there's soap, it gets in their lungs and it's all over."

I love animals. I love animals so much I brought home a pair of cats last year from the shelter. Mama loves animals, too. She grew up hosing dairy cows and picking ticks off her daddy's hunting hounds. That's love, if you ask me. We never had any pets growing up because my sister Juniper is allergic. But now, Junie's at school up in Boston, and as long as I love my cats, which will be forever, they'll live here with me and Mama.

The cats make me mad, sometimes. Junie told me we can all learn from the things that hurt us. And I learn so much from those cats. Their lessons are less complicated than the ones Junie teaches me: I've learned that the armrest of our sofa is made of solid wood. That the vacuum doesn't like it when you hoover up kitty litter. Also, that bleach should never, ever be used to clean up cat pee. The cats are far easier to love than the fleas. I am still trying to learn from the fleas. I am still trying to love them.

Certainly, the fleas love each other. Damned if you can't hear all the fleas getting down, if you know what I mean. Worse than the Dating Game on TV. There's so much love in this house I ache from it. So every morning, before I go to the animal shelter, I sit and breathe in front of the Buddha statue Junie gave me last summer from her trip to India. It's there the fleas greet me. Their bites make me look like I got the pox and I'm glad I'm done with high school because I don't want to hear what everyone else has to say about it.

Junie's been real nice to me ever since she went away to school. Last summer, she sat with me in front of Buddha from India and showed me how to close my eyes and breathe.

"It will make you calm, Shirl," she said. "Return to your breath; you'll find tranquility." I want to be calm like Junie. I want to be tranquil, too, and sometimes I think of her when I sit in front of the Buddha. Sometimes I pretend she's attached a secret camera on him, and so I wear lipstick before I sit down, so I look good, and I try not to slap myself when the fleas bite. I can just see her: she should be doing homework at college, but no, she's watching her big sister on a big screen TV in the lobby of her dorm with all her friends to see if I'm breathing right, to see if I deny love to an animal by hitting a flea. She sent me a picture once of her and her friends in the lobby, and I'd never seen such a huge TV in the background. It would embarrass me, personally, to watch someone I knew on TV like that. But in case any of Junie's friends are boys, I sometimes pull a pillowcase over the Buddha when I undress. I try to follow Mama's orders and, these days, I give it up for no one. Not even on college TV.

Junie told me once at breakfast that I might as well go on and deep-fry the cats if I did not extend my love for animals to the pig who died for my bacon. Mama fries the bacon hard because I ask her to. There's no need to pick through the pile for the good ones if they're all crispy. To eat bacon, Junie said, is not to love all animals, because the pig died for you.

"Isn't tasting good his job?" I'd asked. But I knew even then, before I'd made my full commitment to loving all animals, that I was stalling. I ate the whole plate that day, on account it was Christmas, but I haven't eaten bacon since, at least not when anyone's around, which is hardly ever. Mama keeps a close watch on me. I still think appreciating the pig you eat is a kind of love, too. Like the same way we love Jesus because he died on the cross. But I keep this thought to myself because I don't think it's one Junie would appreciate. And we don't even go to church anymore. And I still have to figure out how to love all animals. That's why I visit the shelter: these are animals I can love. They're always friendly. Their tails wag. Not like the fleas, whose bodies are built like sesame seeds with legs. Some days, I sit in front of the Buddha, or in front of the bathroom mirror and I'll feel the pinch. My right hand stops the left, mid-stroke, and I think, Stop the killing! You are not a battlefield!

But I am a battlefield. I am. Most days, I think about Junie watching me on TV and I let the fleas eat me up. She says it's karma, some cosmic debt, like maybe in another life I was a dog, and I upturned a pullcart of oranges in Tunisia, and all those oranges came back as fleas. Other days, it's all I can do to not pinch one between my finger and thumb, like Mama said, and drown it in one of the dishes of soapy water she's set about the house. I tried it once, had that bugger in my fingers, but I couldn't put it in water. How's that for an animal lover?

I wrote this in a letter to Junie at college, and she called and told me everyone needed to think more like me.

"I love the extent of your love," she said, "but don't let it scare you."

I'm not scared of anything. I just want to learn how to love all animals by finding a way to love the fleas. Sitting in front of the Buddha helps. Sitting in this bathtub helps. Mama added a capful of bubbles for me so I'll smell pretty after. And the fleas don't drown, either. I can see them leaping from my hair for dry land. I asked Junie when she'll come home next, and she said she's not sure. She told me sometimes you need distance to be able to love something fully.

ANNEALED

1. How I lost my fingerprints

The fingerprints went before the split, in the jewelry class, back before
I knew better. Back when I'd imagined that all I needed was a hobby
to occupy my time during those evenings when my husband Wylie was
in North Carolina on a business trip with his business partner. During
those mornings when I'd wake up in a bed built for two and find only
one.

It's embarrassing to admit. In the jewelry class, we took torches to
copper. I'd nearly finished the pendant for a treasure box necklace. The
pendant could hold a tooth or a button or some other small object, like
a miniature shadow box. And I loved the cherry red torch-glow of the
little half-shell vessel I'd made. I loved how luminous transformed ore
could be. Copper: mother to all those pennies and water pipes, mined
from the center of the earth to form the shape of my choosing.

Our instructor had told us how torched heat travels into the interior of the metal, extracting from it the hardening effects of hundreds of hammer blows. And when I turned off the torch, the idiot in me—the one who fails to pay attention, follow instructions, read signs, take advice—reached for the red-hot pendant to douse it in water. As though it hadn't undergone a good 3000 degrees Fahrenheit flame to realign itself, as though the instructor hadn't urged us dozens of times to don gloves, wear goggles, constrain hair, use the tongs provided at every workstation. And thus it came to be that two of my fingertips and the thumb on my left hand got singed, prints seared forever into copper.

It takes but a few screaming moments to get down to raw.

It's the build-back that's the most painful.

2. CELL DIVISION

It was a month after I lost my fingerprints that Wylie left Somerville on business to North Carolina and never came back. Except for the bed, which cannot be cut in two, the apartment contains half of the objects it used to. In May he paid three men to place his half in a rented truck and drive it from Massachusetts to where his grandmother lives in Rocky Mount. It took a day. What remains is kept as he left it. It sits in anthill clusters in every unvacuumed room. Some days I think there's a pattern in these piles that I have yet to discover, some coded message in the chaos he left behind: a box of dried-up mistletoe. A Darth Vader keychain with no keys. Heaps of old clothes and newspapers. Other days, I shuttle to work and from work, and I don't see piles at all. I don't see much of anything.

For three weeks straight, I came to work with old bandages on my fingertips and a box of hankies, a sagging bra and no coffee. At the start of the fourth week, my boss pulled me into his office to talk about taking a break. To talk about washing my hair. I told him I didn't see what typing had to do with washed hair. He said what he wanted was for me to heal my fingers so I could do my job effectively. You see, I type for a living. Hunt and peck on copy can get you fired.

Or close to it. Just yesterday, after the scabs came off, he sent me home. He sent me home in the middle of a meeting, after they fell to the floor in three sturdy flakes, like torn-up bacon. He sent me home after I stopped typing for a moment to pick them up and, without quite realizing it, put one in my mouth.

To fill the silence that followed, my boss invited me to his office and insisted. He said the leave would help put my "house in order." By "house," of course, he meant, "mind." And he meant "order" as in "sort," but it felt more like a command: Leave. You can't ever suggest mental illness in a professional setting. People lose jobs. I guess for some, metaphor works best. Like how my husband says "business partner" to mean his girlfriend.

It can be confusing if you don't see the pattern. It takes a while for me to catch on. So many gray areas for my gray matter. When the brain sings, Wylie used to joke, it is a gray aria.

I've been singing a lot these days: Do-Re-Goddamn-Me.

Goddamn him, too.

But what does it matter? With no job to add to no husband, the sole tether of my Tuesday is my appointment with the burn doctor. I discover the filters for the coffee under a pile of mail and then drink all eight cups with extra sugar. I find today's *Globe* outside with all the others, skip straight to the Style section that claims the eighties are back, and I look through my closet for an era-friendly pale-yellow-midi-stretch and a pair of saddle shoes with striped socks. I pull from a paper bag long destined for Goodwill a too-tight Bangles T-shirt.

The Bangles. It is all I have: my sole sonic sartorial link to the eighties. And with the thought that this could be a day of firsts, I dust off my old tiara from my beauty pageant days, put my panties in my purse instead of on my person, and leave the house. The burn doctor is not amused.

Nor is he amused when I show him my uneaten twinset of scabs and start talking about my work leave. About what he thinks it means to get a "house in order."

"If it is just about housework, I can almost handle that," I tell him.

"But what I learned from my mother is a clean house brings no ease, just an appearance of it."

"Most people need order, Mrs. Burns," the doctor says, and hands me a card with the name of a therapist, "to make functionality feasible. Some just need a housekeeper."

He is not interested in my scabs. Or the copper pendant in which they are kept. Or my Bangles shirt. But he spends a good twenty minutes examining my damaged fingertips, praising their progress. With the scabs gone, the pads of my fingertips are uncommonly smooth and free of ridges. The tips feel tough and numb from the scar tissue, unless you press hard on them. "It's hardly skin," the doctor says. I'll have to be careful until it grows back. "If it grows back," he reminds me. Then he gives me three green banker's finger pads and some ointment. "For protection," he says. "I hope you find the help you need."

The finger pads look like condoms for a well-hung squirrel. This is according to the girl on the skateboard outside the doctor's office. She has seized my palm on a street corner near the T stop to study them. She thinks they are jewelry. Her name is Juniper, she tells me, and wants to know where I got them. She says, "cool," when I tell her that I lost my fingerprints in a jewelry accident. She points to the scattered dark lines on her arms and says she has scars, too, but she won't say how. I am about to board the Red Line home to Porter Square when I notice a second skateboard under her arm. I think of the piles that await me and ask her to teach me to ride.

"Now?" she asks.

"Why do you have two boards?" I ask.

"One for each foot," she says. She looks down at my yellow skirt.

"I can see your pubes," she says.

"I don't have a problem with that," I say, even though the red spreads from my neck across my cheeks.

"I think maybe you do," she says. The streetcar leaves and traffic starts moving again. Juniper looks up at the Don't Walk sign, willing it to change.

"So how about that lesson?" I ask.

"Do you have any money?" she asks. I search in the bottom of my purse and hand her a twenty. We split a stick of Juicyfruit gum.

3. THE FAILURE OF DIAGRAMS

Too much time is wasted doing the things we think other people want us to do. The solar calculator I keep in my purse tells me I have spent almost a third of my life in a cubicle. Nearly a decade contained indoors, wearing sweaters and square-toed shoes, married to a man with business in another state. Fending off other men who didn't care about the ring on my finger. Until I quit when I was fourteen, my mother had me in on the beauty pageant circuit, convinced that looks alone could get me into college.

Sometimes I hate my mother for her assumptions. And sometimes I think she's right.

Sometimes I wish I could run a diagnostic on my life, inputting my demographic variables (U.S. Census data, political views, Nielsen ratings, credit rating, geography), my skills (social and technical and sexual), and my past mistakes (see above) that could tabulate a best-shot diagram for future optimal living. I'd get back a customized list that would indicate what to keep and what to purge:

Jarred Pasta Sauce: Purge.

Pat Sajak: Purge.

Artichokes: Keep.

Sea glass: Keep.

Coconut popsicles: Keep.

No doubt the diagnostic would show that—in spite of my propensity for physical injury—skateboarding without underwear racks up dozens of points, like nailing a quadruple Lutz. The judges would have to give a ten in all categories: Never attempted. Daring act. Danger element. Wardrobe change. Unconventional transport. Divergent sexual dynamic.

But as Juniper spots me across the vacant basketball court, her hand pulling mine on our twin boards, her left foot supplying the momentum for us both, I realize points don't matter to this kind of joy. To diagram it is to negate the qualities that make it so. Still, I panic when we pass the foul line. I cannot turn and I cannot stop. At the lip of the court she leaps, fearless, onto the lawn. I follow. She has taught me how to fall. The grass catches us, turns our scraped skin green. She rolls on her back, closer to me.

I ask her to tell me about herself. She says she is twenty. That she travels solely by T and by board. That she dyed parts of her hair green last week because she wanted to be one with the trees. That she'd just come from Jamaica Plain to ferret out the best deal on her weed. She shows me her bag of buds as if it were a prize, tucked next to a four-pack of Phillies in the zippered fuzzy ear of her Hello Kitty backpack.

"Those JP lesbians are always game to split a deal for girl favors," she says.

She snaps a match against her board's deck and lights a blunt. I'm her second girl today, she informs me, as she sits upright, leans in. But her first kiss.

Mine, too. I couldn't give a shit about the other girl. I want Juniper, I realize, but not quite in the way her actions suggest she wants me. Still, currents strong and bright flash in the spaces between us, uncapturable but present, like the glow of sparklers trailing at night. They are fueled by laughter and sensual sighs that originate in the inner part of the knee, and travel upward. They cross and surge. They push outward, up the torso and into the lungs. In the ebb exhales carbon monoxide. In the ebb is damp hands and saliva pooling in the bottom of the mouth. Between the ebb and the surge to the next flow is the tense rush of hot blood that gathers at my very base.

"You ever done this before?" she asks.

"Done what?" I ask in a way that she understands to mean No. Too often sex is the default activity for what is, at its core, an attraction of character. But right now, I want whatever Juniper can offer. I want her to see evidence of my wanting in the placement of my hands against my stomach, how my green knee falls lazily toward the lawn. How I let my fingers push gently through her uncombed hair, braided in places and honeybrown at the roots. I try taming her green locks like I might a child's. And compared to me, she is a child.

Or is she? I feel heat in my chest and wonder about her breasts, packed in purple pinstripes as though all muscle, no bounce. Unimaginable, even when I was her age. Growing up, my friends and I would inherit our mothers' old hand-me-down underwires, loose and slack and silky soft and nearly gray from overuse, the adjustable straps twisted and frayed from the wash. Today, the bras are pink and lacy black and tennis white and plaid and posies. Today, the bras seal in, contain, bustle up and solidify all that is soft beneath. Maybe this is what her bra does, why she is ten years younger than me but seems so much older.

She takes my left hand and asks, "So what's with this green thumb gig?"

"Does it matter?" I say.

"No. Just trying to figure you out," she says.

"Impossible."

"Not really," she says. "A jewelry accident?" She removes the banker's pads from my fingers and thumb and studies the ridgeless skin beneath. She touches each of my fingers with her pinkie. To look at this girl, you'd think she has never once contemplated cubicles. I don't ask. To ask would make her mind travel into those closed spaces of offices: a world of overdressed bodies and the objects of production: all of it partitioned, sectioned, clusters of people and plastic and microprocessors on overdrive.

"My husband left me," I say.

"Good for him," she says.

"What the hell?"

"Good for you, too," she says. "Why stick around if you're not happy?"

"But I was happy," I say. "We were. I thought."

"If you aren't sure, then you probably weren't," she says.

"Thanks a lot," I say.

"Except pain, how can you be sure about anything?" She gives my pointer finger a good pinch and I cry out. The burn doctor would not be amused.

"*I like a look of agony,*" she says, "*because I know it's true.*"

"What do you know about it?"

"Plenty." She reaches again for my fingers, but I have tucked them into a fist. "Want to see the scabs?" I ask. "They're in my purse."

"No."

Juniper returns my hand to my stomach and moves hers under my skirt to gauge my reaction to her mouth on mine. Her fingertips are inexplicably cool as they web around my inner thigh. Her other hand braces herself against the grass. A human lean-to, she is, a small balancing act just toppled from a skateboard.

"Making sense of anything is like trying to get to the end of Pi. It's impossible," I say. She uses both hands now to pin me in the grass and I enjoy the resistance of my shoulders against the pressure of her touch before I will myself to it. But I find myself thinking about my lost fingerprints. Of the green pads that are no longer on my fingers, and are now on hers. My tiara that's just fallen onto the grass.

"You think too much about shit that doesn't matter," she says. She puts the tiara on her green locks. "Husband or no husband. Let it go. You don't need any of it. Just feel."

At this point, I'm too stripped to know what I need. Whether I'm getting to my core by moving my hips against a pair of sticky fingers in a public park, or if in doing so, I'm adding to the fray of amalgams. What would all of this look like to a passer-by: the green grass, the skateboards, my mouth on Juniper's neck and her hand up my skirt? I can just hear my mother: Oh, so you're a lesbian now? Or a cop: You're under arrest for sexual misconduct. My husband: Finally!

"What's so funny?" she wants to know. Her fingers press against me. My giggle turns to gasp as the wisdom of extremes hits me: pain or pleasure is where the purity resides. Wholeness exists in the creation and the ruination. And I have never failed to create my own ruin.

"You sure you don't want to see my scabs?" I ask.

"I have already seen them," she says.

4. Physics and chemistry in a park

When she is finished with me, Juniper says it's time for lunch, even though it's nearly three. She hands me what's left of the snuffed blunt and says she's going to track down the hot dog vendor we'd passed earlier. She asks what I want on my dog and I inhale deep and say ketchup and mustard and relish if they have it.

"Stay right there," she says. The plastic wheels of her board make skipping sounds from the squares of sidewalk as she gains momentum. When the skipping sounds dissolve, the void of alone sets in and I sit up to find the other skateboard gone. My purse, gone.

It's a strange feeling to have finished an orgasm; it's the relief from the relief of isolation, a restoration of back to normal. Only it's the relief from the nexus of pleasure, saturated and candy-sweet.

And how unfair is it that the person who has given you such pleasure takes with her everything else: no keys no money no T pass no newspaper no trashy romance novel no underwear no list of Things to Do no credit cards no copper vessel necklace no scabs no calculator no business card for the divorce lawyer no pamphlet on birth control no green banker's pads no way of telling what will happen now that the effects that have made me have been stuffed into a Hello Kitty backpack, on the smooth shoulders of a beautiful twenty-year-old in a purple bra with green hair and fingers that smell like me, blunt-high on her skateboard.

The park here has leather-bottomed swings. I rise from the grass, clutching the blunt, and place it between my lips. I sit on the swing, and pump it until I soar. Then I let go, return to earth tumbling, and climb to the top of the nearby slide. There I spy the roundabout. The sweat from my thighs makes the aluminum squeal on the slide down. I approach the roundabout, test the sturdiness of its red metal railings before I grab one and start to run. I run for nearly a minute, training my eyes on the corrugated metal platform, the sandy footprints of children, and stiff, black gum too viscous to be a threat.

I hoist myself onto the platform and lie on my back, clutching the iron pole. And because today the sky holds no clouds, it seems fixed, and the world is a blur of trees and grass and parked cars and jungle gyms. My head feels heavy every time I raise it. So I close my eyes and let the spinning soothe me, pressing into mudra my now-naked finger against my now-naked thumb, pushing from my mind the piles I must contend with at home. Pushing from my mind the unopened mail and the likelihood that the spare key is locked inside the apartment. Instead, I wonder what of me Juniper was feeling before she fled. Then it occurs to me that I never once had that thought about my husband. But I think about it now, and as the roundabout slows, I move my left hand under my hemline to discover my undoing. I reach in deep and reclaim what remains of all that I have lost.

AZIMUTH AND ALTITUDE

You have reached the home of Juniper Weaver. Please leave a message after the tone.

JUNIE? IT'S SHIRL. Don't think for a minute Mama doesn't know it was you snitching at the butter again. It couldn't be anyone else. She called me just now and told me what you were up to. Asked if I could talk sense into you. You, a grown woman, still sneaking butter from Mama's fridge.

I guess you decided not to stay at home with her tonight up on Penny Hill, even though I couldn't be there, me all laid up at the doctor's with my broken leg. It's a shame because I bet she'd have liked you to sit out on the porch with her. I bet you'd have liked it, too. It's the only time of day when she doesn't talk. I remember when we were little, how we'd look out over the hillside at the red blinking lights from those towers. Do you remember those names we'd give them? Fire, Zap, Power, Blinky. They're so pretty, all red and twinkling, blinking at us in the dark, winking up at the airplanes like barmaids or something. And those times when a plane did fly by at night, we'd yell up at the pilots not to hit the towers, even though those planes flew so high at night you could have stacked one tower on the other and it would never hit.

For a long time, when we were really little, you thought those lights were red stars. Then you decided they were planets, then fireflies. Firelights, you called them, and you'd reached toward them and once you nearly fell off the porch. You were all clean from our bath, smelling like talc in your pajamas with the plastic soles that made your feet sweat. Your hands were so small then. And you'd reach out and those lights would blink off every time you tried and sometimes you'd cry cause you could never get 'em. And this one time, Pa came out to smoke and you asked him, "What are those firelights?" And he said, "They's beacons."

"Like a bird's nose?" you asked, because you were too little then, and I guess I was, too, to know what a beacon was. It made sense for you to think: Bird's Nose, when you heard the word beacon, even though everyone knows beaks aren't noses. And me, I thought he'd said bacon, and I laughed and laughed at the idea of bacon flaming red on a tower. I breathed a little deeper, pretending maybe I'd smell it sizzling in the night sky. Oh, I know you're thinking, Of course you'd be thinking of bacon, Shirl. What with that baby fat still with me some thirty years later. As Mama says, Junie, my stomach comes first. I've stopped blaming her for overfeeding me all those years. I figure it's the one way she can show me her love.

You have reached the home of Juniper Weaver. Please leave a message after the tone.

IF YOU'RE LISTENING TO THIS MESSAGE, I know you're probably blushing by now. You always turn red every time I say those old words we used to use, like Bird's Nose and Bacon and Baby Fat, like I know you probably blushed when Mama asked if you snitched butter from the fridge.

I understand how you can't help how you are. I guess it's natural for you to want butter, like it's natural for me to want bacon and sugar and the skins of fried chicken and all the things the doctor tells me not to eat. I guess I've got Pa's genes. But I wonder about you and the butter, sometimes, because when we went to see you at that first apartment you had over in Mount Olive when you came home after college—it must have been six years ago now because Pa had driven us there—do you remember how I kept drinking all that cold water from your fridge? You kept saying stuff like, "Boy, Shirley, there's no camel in all Arabia with more water in him than you!" And I laughed because I could just imagine my head and a camel's body, the big solid hump full of water, caravanning some genie Arabian princess through the desert.

I admit I drank all that water because I was curious about the butter. And we weren't three minutes on the freeway home after we had to leave because Pa kept breaking things in the living room, when my bladder gave its four-alarm warning and Pa had to pull off the road and I had to drop it all behind the sign for Beulaville. I still think of all the people on the highway that day who saw me squatting with my pants around my ankles. I still have it in my head that, some day, when I'm in town, or out at the grocery store, a cute boy with a nice red convertible will come up to me and say, "Hey, I think I saw you once, up on I-40? Near the Beulaville exit?" 'Cause if he drove by all that and still liked what he saw and thought to go out of his way to find me and to mention it, maybe my search for your butter would have a point.

You have reached the home of Juniper Weaver. Please leave a message after the tone.

BUT THE FUNNY THING IS, is that I don't recall seeing a single block of butter in your fridge. Not next to the Chinese takeout containers, not in the egg bin, not behind the box of salad, the box of juice, the box of milk, the box of wine. So many boxes. The soy sauce and relish. All those pill bottles. But no butter. I thought at first maybe you'd eaten it all before we got there. And then I thought it was strange because I thought for sure it was your favorite food. I know that if I had my own place, for sure I'd load up my cabinets with the Cap'n Crunch, bacon and eggs, fried chicken, and butterscotch Moon Pies.

But then here is Mama calling me at the hospital, calling me when the doctors say I should be resting, and all she can do is complain about your tine marks in the butter. I told her she should pay more attention to you and less to the butter, seeing how little you get to visit. I told her, "Give Junie the whole stick if she wants it," but you know her. Waste not, and all that. And I know you— you'd never admit you so much as took a lick of that butter. Still the fork tines is telltale you, but I didn't say that to Mama because it would confirm everything and you and I have never been ones to tell on each other.

You have reached the home of Juniper Weaver. Please leave a message after the tone.

DO YOU REMEMBER THAT NIGHT WE COULDN'T SLEEP and we snuck into the pantry and Mama caught you swigging vinegar from the bottle and me eating my tenth packet of the travel sugar that Meemaw used to collect from the IHOP after church on Sundays? Mama in her nighttime curlers and julep mask so bright you could nearly see her face in the dark, like a green skeleton head as she came toward us, and she said she knew what kind of people we'd turn out to be based on the food we stole from the pantry. I got the feeling even then that she used the word "stole" for effect, like it was funny to her or something, her two daughters swilling vinegar, eating sugar. She never did tell us what vinegar said about you, sugar me. And I asked her once and she said she didn't remember ever saying that. It's like hearing that a fortuneteller got news for you, and then she never gives it out, tells you she forgot the fortune. Don't you ever wonder what she really thinks about us? Sometimes from what she says to me, I think she wishes you'd stayed at home instead, that I'd left. But that makes no sense, to waste all your brains and your good body to look after some old lady, even if she is your mother. You're the one with the chance of finding a husband, not me. And I know you have told me time and again that you like girls, and that it's a natural thing for two women to fall in love. And I believe it. I just can't help Mama to understand it 'cause all she wants is a grandchild and I don't think she sees me as mothering material. And I was hopeful when you finally came home from Boston and moved uptown because I thought maybe we'd all be together like old times. But instead, you're all busy with teaching painting, meditating on some cloud somewhere, and loving women instead of men. And making no babies.

Say what you want about Mama, after all these years she's still sharp enough to note the tine marks in the butter.

Even though I asked one of the nurses, there's no room in the hospital that faces the hillside and I feel a little sad on account of it. I've been here going on three days and I never thought I'd miss going out on the front porch at home to watch those red lights. I still count the seconds between each blink, like we used to do when we were little, try to catch the pattern from one red tower light to the next. If you'd bothered to stay at home with Mama tonight, you'd have seen that they added two new towers, up toward the north. You'd have seen that they blink at the same time once every hour. But just once.

You have reached the home of Juniper Weaver. Please leave a message after the tone.

I KNOW THERE'S BEEN A LOT OF TALK ABOUT THIS BROKEN LEG OF MINE, and I'll just tell you about it directly so you won't wonder. So, I was sitting out on the porch, and it was so dark and pretty and I was just enjoying those red lights, and the real stars. The air was really clean, too, like the breeze carried whiffs of something alive in the hillside and it was making its rounds to all the neighbors. And I saw a little golden light turn on, right near the base of the fire tower, and the first thing I thought was: fire at the fire tower. But it was just a porch light, or a campfire, or something, because it didn't move or grow or anything. But it got me thinking that if someone lived in the fire tower, or even near it, and they cared to look southways toward us, they'd never know we lived here. And it seems unfair, don't you think, that we could be so aware of these towers, these lights, for practically our whole lives and that no one living near them would ever know about us back. That to them, we'd be just part of that landscape of rolling black—part of, I don't know, the great nothing the world becomes around here at night, except for these red points of light that shine and glow and wink up at those airplane pilots.

So it got me thinking: what if you realized you could shine but you chose not to? That all you had to do to get noticed was to flip a switch and the whole world, if it cared to look, could see you, could know you were alive? Fireflies have been mating that way for years. It's how they find love. So why not make the effort? Maybe some love will come out of it, right? It's like how you know someone has been around, by the clues they leave behind. Like how I know you've been home when the butter block no longer looks like the last thing to touch it was a butter knife.

So what I did was find the lights from all the Christmas boxes in the attic. I started with the crepe myrtle. Then the mailbox, the porch. The lower branches of the magnolia, even though I know we've been saying for years it needs to be cut. That's when I thought about the rabbit ears up top the house. You can't deny it would make our part of the constellation here on the hill a whole lot brighter. Maybe the pilots will look down from their 747s or their Cessnas and see our glow and they'll think, There's the golden Eye of the Mewborn Andromeda. There's the tip of the handle of the Big Little Dipper!

Well, sorry for me that it all backfired. Sorry for me that I didn't think about waiting until daylight to make the house glow, that I didn't think how the roof would be slick with nighttime dew, that I'd slip off it and break my leg and bust my elbow. After that old ladder fell on me, my left eye looks like the shiner you gave me in middle school when you found out that I'd given my underwear to the seventh-grade boys, and they stuck it on your head during health class. I am still sorry for that, sorry you had to smell my privates on your person. I could not have predicted that would happen. I know we said we forgave each other, but strange things happen sometimes and they never leave you.

Like when you cut yourself open, and you're fine after, mostly, but the scar still stays, and you can't help but run your finger over and over it, to remind yourself that you're not hurt anymore. And it's true. Even with the scars you can't see: you're not hurt anymore, but you can't forget, either, but there's no place to put your finger as a reminder. I was always grateful you never told mom I gave my underwear to the boys that day, even though I wasn't sure if it was because you were too ashamed, or because we were a Secret Sister team, that something special united us, just like something special united our parents. Mama never would answer any question we asked until she'd talked it out first with Pa. And it's not like dad was any king of judgment, the way he got so out of control with his six packs and his smokes, like those times when he rushed at you in the dark, and all you could see was the glowing ash coming from his mouth, smell the trail of smoke coming from his clothes, his hair. I was glad for that cigarette because even though I hated his smoking, you could never otherwise tell where he was headed. Those cigarettes saved us. I think about it now and maybe even if we were a Secret Sister team back then, that maybe you were ashamed of me deep down, ashamed of our family. Like how Pa used to chase you around the yard like that, was nearly the same thing as me handing out my underwear to the boys, that it held up some sort of mirror about who we were, that maybe we weren't the perfect and loving and helpful family of four that Mama likes to keep framed on top of the television set. All of us wore some shade of red the day that picture was taken because it brought out how blonde we all were.

You have reached the home of Juniper Weaver. Please leave a message after the tone.

Last I saw, you'd dyed your hair purple and called it eggplant. And you know my hair is kind of an ugly blonde-brown now. "The color of blah," Mama likes to say. She still clips coupons from the Sunday paper and sets them on my breakfast plate every time she sees one for a Nice 'n' Easy discount. But I heard those hair chemicals can give you cancer, and there's no sense killing yourself over self-improvement, even if I was inclined to go blondie-blonde like it used to be. It seems silly to think those people in the picture are the people we are today. Pa's not even around to compare it to. Sometimes I go visit him behind the house. Sometimes I kick his gravestone because we both know he deserves it. And sometimes I cry about him being gone.

I remember Pa once told me I must have been a mariner in another life, always looking for the lights to guide me. One Christmas he made me a present of a map of the lighthouses along the coast. It was the only gift he ever gave me. I think he got it that time he went on that fishing trip to Hatteras with his friends. If you care to look next time you visit, the map is still right next to all your postcards from India, on our old bedroom wall. I memorized the shape and stripe of each lighthouse a long time ago. They're like codes so you know where you are on the ocean, without having to ask anyone outright. And they're all black or white, so you can make out their pattern even at night. And I was thinking maybe someday we could take a raft or rowboat together out to the ocean. We could start at the very tip of Hatteras, down at the Frying Pan Shoals and row all the way up to the Currituck Lighthouse in Corolla. And we could sleep all day in the sun and row at night, with the help of a lantern. And all those lighthouse tenders would see our little light and flash us a signal now and again, in Morse Code or whatever they use to send their messages. We'd have to learn it. There's no secrets you could keep on the water if you know the code. I wonder if any of those tenders ever thought to tell a joke to those old sailors using the lighthouse light to guide their boats in the dark. I guess it would be hard to tell a joke using the light from a lighthouse. Can you imagine, sending out the punchline, letter by letter? You'd probably figure it out before they'd be done the spelling. Pa liked to say, "Jokes got to come quick or not at all." I might not make a good lighthouse tender. They must spend a lot of time alone. And I know I'd be craggy if I never got to tell a good joke now and again, even if I had to tell it slowly and in code form. History shows you don't laugh at any jokes anymore, and Mama laughs at anything, as long as I tell her beforehand it's a joke.

But we had a few good times, didn't we? Those quiet nights on the porch, swapping the knock-knocks in the dark, watching the lights blink, me playing Meemaw's fiddle sometimes, and then, after Pa broke my hand, and then the fiddle, not at all. Then there were just the lights.

But see, now, how the lights brought you back home, even though you probably would have preferred to stay in your little vacuum far away from us, with that woman friend of yours, and leave us be on the hillside. The good part in all this, of me falling, is that at least I was at the tail end of stringing up those lights. All we have to do, you know, when I get home from the hospital, is to find the extension cord from the shed and plug it in. I hope you can come and get me. I may be ready as early as tomorrow, the doctors say, and with you living uptown, it wouldn't be too much for you to come get me when it's dark. And we don't have to talk much to each other, because I know how you like it quiet. But you know I'd like to see what the tower lights look like from another view. And then it will all come back, as we drive the road to our house, all those good and familiar feelings of home, all the tower lights placed just so, like we've known them to be since we were babies in feetie pajamas talking about birds' noses and bacon.

Maybe you'll help me find that old extension cord, and we can plug it in together, and we can join the rest of those hillside lights, our one small bright point in the dark. I bet when you drive away, you'll be able to see home from your rearview mirror, and you'll see all our old Christmas lights on the rabbit ears, the weather vane, the chimney, blinking at you along with the tower lights, to remind you, like in code, with no words at all: We're here. We're here. And when you get home, I'd love it if you could call me and let me know if it works, if you can really see our lights glowing in the dark, out there with all the others.

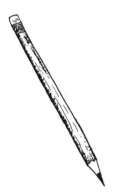

OBJECT LESSONS

IN THE REMOTEST REGION OF BIHAR, on the dustiest of backstreets of Bodh Gaya, dozens of children surrounded Juniper as she attempted to track down what she hoped was their school. But no one could tell her, exactly, where to find it. Still, little boys in hand-me-down soccer shirts, big sisters with babies hoisted on their hips, and a gaggle of other cheerful kids skipped and chattered alongside her, chanting "school!" or "Michael Jackson!" or "Hello, madam!" in steady, repetitive ribbons of sound, a record of all the English words they'd picked up and internalized in their relatively short lives. Snot invariably crusted just above their wide smiles; some had eyes rimmed with kohl, like the hollows of jubilant skeleton heads, absorbing and reflecting the summer sun. Their hands were filthy from a day's worth of play, except for traces of shimmery pink on their fingernails, a treat from some other Western tumbleweed who'd delighted in applying girly-pink polish, each tiny digit now the sole remainder of the visitor's fading and transient attention.

But Juniper had not brought with her nail polish but rather sixteen dozen pencils to offer the local kids, although she had plenty of finger lacquer back in her studio in Boston. She loved the possibilities of a simple single pencil and a sheet of paper gave her, for nearly nothing. Ever since her first term in art school, she'd decided on principle to buy only inexpensive and scrap art supplies, spurred by the expectation that she'd actually pay forty dollars for a tube of phthalo blue paint. Her aesthetic of "cheap art" scavengery helped to establish her voice and vision as a collage artist: trafficking in discarded tar paper and turpentine, charcoal briquettes and corrugated cardboard and ancient magazines and peculiar packaging culled from the recycling bin, yarn from old sweaters, X-rays, thrift shop ledgers and photos: all of it trimmed and pasted and hand-stitched together in a desire to take the old and discarded and to make it new. Make it relevant. Make it Art. And, of course, in India, she'd found no shortage of newspaper clippings filled with tightly-kerned Devanagari and bright placards of Hindu deities that graced the grills of Tata trucks or advertised themselves as serene guardians on packaging for sandalwood soap or bags of rice. She'd save each scrap of color or texture as the fodder for future collages, tuck it all away in a plastic sleeve, feeling a bit like a bird gathering scraps, piece by piece, for its messy, haphazard nest.

Freshly kicked out of her study abroad summer ashram program for an unfortunate and spectacularly public run-in with illicitly procured ganja and a large bottle of Tuborg, Juniper decided to take the first train bound for Bodh Gaya—the Center of the Universe, she'd heard more than once. Suddenly solo and in a village that felt more like a city, given the legions of monks and nuns and pilgrims from all over the world who'd staked a claim at the site of the historic Buddha's enlightenment, Juniper decided it was time to make good on her pencil delivery to a local elementary school. She'd lugged the gleaming golden Dixon Ticonderogas all the way from Boston, sharpened each one herself, and welled with pride, thinking about her standing in front of a classroom amid rows of perfectly aligned desks, every child clutching a brand-new pencil, notebooks open, following her in lockstep as she drew on the chalkboard the petals on a flower, the trunk of an elephant, each of their names in English. Saheli. Arjun. Maya.

"All things start with an idea written on the page," Juniper liked to say to her classmates. "Poems. Songs. Designs. Art. Image. Blueprints. Two hundred pencils is two hundred possibilities. Two hundred poems or camels or robots or whatever."

During the crowded train ride to Gaya, Juniper overheard a few other Western passengers discussing the Kali Bandits, throngs of men who, as devotees of the Hindu Goddess of Death, would roll out a massive log onto the lone connector road to Bodh Gaya in the middle of the night, and then attack any vehicle unfortunate enough to be traveling that route after dark.

"Sure, let's blame the goddess for their looting," Juniper had said to the other travelers, whose expressions told her the Kali Bandits were nothing to joke about. But she saw no logs or bandits as the tiny bus rolled into town midday and, after she'd settled into a closet sized-room at the cheapest hostel she could find, she unpacked her things and decided to find the village school.

"School?" she asked the children. They nodded. "Yes! School?" they repeated. But then her question "Where?" was met with giggles for an answer, peals of laughter ringing through the street. The hostel clerk gave her a simple, "School? Down the road. That way." She'd walked "that way," which happened to be toward the marketplace, just outside the sacred grounds of the bodhi tree. But still, no school. As she continued her search, she amassed the presence of even more children and it was all she could do not to dole out the pencils then and there on the street. But Juniper's vision of herself inside a classroom, as Teacher, stopped her.

"School?" she asked a street-side tailor. He pointed her in the same direction as the hotel clerk, never once looking up from his work, the needle of his elegant vintage machine simultaneously puncturing and joining delicate strips of ruby-hued silk. She picked up a scrap of castoff silk and slipped it in her pocket.

For the first time, as she traveled solo, with no tether and no one here who knew her, Juniper felt like maybe she'd be able to start over fresh. For years she'd craved anonymity. Solitude. She'd sought to exist where no one knew her name, or where she grew up, or anything about her that she didn't want them to know. She wanted to remember this feeling—of being no one from nowhere—when she returned to Boston, or to Mewborn, where everyone seemed to know her a little too well, knew her in ways that she did not want to be known. *Who are you?* she'd ask herself every morning, as she attempted to sit on a cushion before dawn, trying to void her rollercoaster thoughts, to void herself as the world knew her, to reprogram the makeup of her decidedly selfish and on-the-take attitude. *Who are you, she'd ask herself, and who can you become, when no one knows who you are?* She thought she'd found the start of an answer when she first arrived in Varanasi—to sit in an ashram and do nothing but try not to think—but perhaps the answer was here in the streets, responding in the moment to the logistics of travel, to the play and joy present in the children who trailed her, to enjoy the walk to the village school as much as the act of donating to the school itself.

The postcards she'd send back home to Mewborn every week were for the sole purpose of letting Shirley and Ma know that she was still alive, that she hadn't got taken in by some "cult of crazies" as Ma had so delicately put it. But they were so wrapped up in their own little world of sitcoms and ancient magazines and animal rescue that Juniper often wondered whether the postcards home even mattered. Or was it simply a painful reminder, for Shirl especially, who'd been a bit "off" after Ma dropped her headfirst on the porch, of the life that she'd grown into on Penny Hill, that Juniper was living a life Shirl would never have?

It was no secret Juniper never quite fit in with the Ma and Shirl Show. The waist-high stacks of egg cartons and magazines guarding the entryway, the unopened mail and undusted furniture and the hazy rabbit-ears Sylvania, to say nothing of the stores of inedible food that no one ever threw away, always seemed like a physical extension of their family's inner chaos. And later, when Juniper got to college, her art projects taught her how to order the chaos, to make meaning of the stacks of objects Ma refused to toss. The collages she'd make from curbside finds and Oodles of Noodles packaging and Sears catalogs, 550 miles away from home, helped shift her perspective, and she returned to Mewborn for winter break ready to embrace her people and her past. To be curious about it rather than rail against it. But the ancient stagnant scent of home confronted her as soon as she stepped through the threshold. The same food sat rotting in the fridge since she'd last seen it. And then there were the pair of cats whose dander seized upon her sinuses.

The next morning, hopped up on non-drowsy Benadryl, Juniper woke before dawn and decided that, instead of complaining, she'd choose to help with the clutter situation. As Ma and Shirl slept, Juniper spent the morning hauling garbage bags brimming with age-old cartons of milk, mystery leftovers, stalks of rotting vegetables and a more than a few long-expired and crusted-over bottles of Texas Pete's. In addition to the mealy-bugged flour sacks and expired boxes of Rice-A-Roni, Juniper found the red velvet cake box mix Ma promised to make for her 16th birthday. Juniper paused from her purge as a pang of nostalgia, or something like it, welled up. Surprised by how a seemingly innocuous box of cake mix could amass value, hold a memory, mean something, Juniper brought it to her bedroom and tucked it into her backpack.

As Juniper wiped down every shelf and countertop with bleach, and mopped and vacuumed the floor, she felt proud she could improve Ma and Shirl's quality of life in this ratty little house they all called home. Love through action, she thought, tossing the stacks of *Redbooks* and *Better Homes* into boxes, setting aside a few interesting looking *McCall's* and Sears catalogs for her collages, anticipating how glad Ma would be when she found the kitchen bright and tidy.

Instead, as she returned from the curb to drop off the last box of magazines, she heard, "What she done done with all our food?" And there launched an hours-long tirade and a torrent of accusations about stealing magazines and sneaking around and the money wasted by tossing "perfectly good food" and all the rest of it. Juniper wasn't sure how her good intentions got so twisted in her mother's mind. It was as though she'd somehow removed a part of Ma's brain that morning and tossed it out onto the curb. And about an hour into the tirade, Juniper startled as it hit her: there was nothing she could do that would make Ma happy. She could have bought her a brand-new house and Ma would complain that it wasn't her old one. *It doesn't matter what I do,* Juniper thought, *if everything I do upsets her. So I can do what I want.* For the first time in her life, even as Ma raved on, her voice ricocheting through the neighborhood, and Shirl cowering on the front porch, yelling for them to stop, Juniper finally felt free.

ACCOMPANIED NOW BY AN ENTIRE SCHOOL'S WORTH OF CHILDREN, Juniper came across a small white cement building off the main dirt road and down a footpath. The children pointed and yelled "school! school!" But the heavy metal door was barred shut and padlocked. Through the bars on the window, Juniper spotted a few rows of bench desks, a cracked green chalkboard. A single naked bulb dangled from the ceiling. The kids looked up at her, expectant.

"School?" she asked.

"School!" the children responded, gleeful. Thumbs up. Mission accomplished. For show, she tried to open the door, then pantomimed a questioning gesture—arms bent at the elbows, palms up. "Why closed?" she asked. The kids chattered with each other in Hindi before one boy burst out, "No School, madam… Summer!"

Juniper sighed. Of course. It was, after all, July. She glanced inside the school once more, feeling the brunt of the sun on her peeling forehead, the weight of two hundred pencils in her shoulder bag. It was time to part ways with her entourage and recenter, to retool her plan to teach these children how to find their creativity. She walked further into the center of the village as the children, still chattering and laughing, pulled at her clothes, their tiny hands forming a massive daisy chain. Not far from the school, the pinging ring of what sounded like ice cream truck music filtered through the air. But it wasn't an ice cream truck, but rather, a large man operating the smallest functioning Ferris wheel Juniper had ever seen. He was charging children a pisa each for a few go-arounds on his hand-made contraption, fabricated precariously from welded sheet metal and spare bolts and a mishmash of technicolor paint. An erector set on steroids. There was no motor. To make the ride work, another man hung from a lever on the Ferris wheel, leaping then pulling, again and again, using the force of his weight against the contraption as pairs of children sat hip to hip in the tiny booths, laughing with each jolt.

The children with Juniper stood spellbound by the Ferris wheel, clamoring for a pisa so they too could ride it, and Juniper could not help but think that this rickety contraption, though genius in its own right, wouldn't pass any safety inspector's code back home. She had no small change but then remembered her pencils. *Maybe I don't need a school,* she thought. *I'll rip out pages from my journal and make a school right here.* And without a second thought, she reached into her shoulder bag and clutched a good fistful of pencils, ready to dole them out one by one as the Ferris wheel continued its cycle. But she barely had time to pull the pencils from her bag when she was inundated by children, who somehow understood, as all children do, when someone was giving something away. The Ferris wheel was all but forgotten as news of the golden 2B Ticonderogas spread, and within seconds, every last pencil in her bag was gone, her journal, gone and torn to shreds. But it did not stop the tiny, pencil-wielding hands from seeking out more. Juniper hoisted her bag above the children's reach as they reached up and swarmed her, stabbing at each other, and then at her, with the pencils' sharp tips. She couldn't escape, and huddled into herself, protecting her torso from the gouging, as it hit her that nothing she could offer these children could satisfy what they actually needed. Not a pencil. Not a pisa. No amount of rupees or clothing or flip-flops or tissues or hairbrushes or bananas or nail polish. Not anything in her now-empty shoulder bag or in her luggage at the hostel or in her dorm room in Boston.

The children continued to stab at Juniper's arms and hands, and stabbed other kids' hands who wanted pencils, stabbed at pink lacquered fingertips that already clutched pencils but wanted more, stabbed at anything moving in this throng of destructive energy and desire. Juniper could not escape the chaos she'd created, could not tamp the shouting and the stabbing and the crying and sound of wood snapping as the stabbing and screaming continued and she imagined the ironic smirk that would come with the news back home if she were to be pulled under and trampled to death by a stampede of children and their pencils just down the street from the Center of the Universe. Murdered by her own idiot idealism. Teaching kids how to draw. What was she thinking?

Just then, the Ferris wheel man's assistant leapt from his perch, grabbed a broom, and swooped it across the crowd of kids. He did not strike, but every kid felt the force of air pushing overhead and ducked. The second warning swoop worked, as the children unwillingly parted from the throng, their desire for pencils trumped by the prospect of getting swept away by the butt of a broom. Juniper called out an insufficient *"Dhanyabad!"* to the Ferris wheel man as she fled the crowd of children, tromping over dozens of broken pencils. A few kids clutched their pencils and continued to follow her, yelling "Madam!" "Fuck you!" "Pisa! Rupee!" "I love you!" in the thrill of the chase of a crazy white lady.

Down the twist and turns of yet another dusty alley, past the tailor who continued to sew his silk and past the bangle vendor whose thin metal bands shone like jewels, Juniper found herself gasping for air outside the doorway of a tiny statue shop. She could feel the heat of the day rise and surge as she took stock of the pencil scrapes welting her arms and hands. A small red stool beckoned from a darkened corner of the shop and she sat down as the last of the children, still in hot pursuit, raced past. She'd tried to do right by these kids, and where did it get her? Maybe living in the moment isn't all it's cracked up to be, she thought. Maybe transformation is a bullshit myth. Maybe Juniper would always, at her core, be forced to be herself. That her nature was her own, and no journey to Boston or India or anywhere else would change that.

As Juniper caught her breath, her eyes adjusted to the shelves of soapstone and wooden carvings of nearly every Hindu god—Siva and Ganesha, Krishna playing the flute, Sarasvati with her veena and Durga riding a tiger, but no sign of Kali, her long tongue sticking out, a necklace of human skulls adorning her neck. She thought of the goddess's devotees rolling out the massive log in the dead of night, willing to scavenge whatever they could from a van of wayward pilgrims. How do you ever come to decide that blocking a road with a log to loot and murder people is a good idea? Or, for that matter, smashing a bottle of beer against the wall of an ashram? Or refusing to toss food years past the expiration date?

On the shelves closest to Juniper, from floor to ceiling, sat dozens of identical serene Buddhas, man upon man upon sitting stone man. How many Buddhas in the world have there actually been? And how many could there be, Juniper wondered, if any of us chose to simply sit and sit and sit? Juniper reached up and held one of the buddhas in her hand, feeling its stony coolness, its satisfying weight, and placed it on the pencil gash on her left forearm. She stared down at its beatific gaze as it soothed her wound, and wondered how long the real Buddha actually sat in front of that famous tree before he felt something fundamental shift within him. But, as she slipped the stone Buddha into her shoulder bag, she knew that, for her, today was not that day.

Just then, a creaky, melodic voice filtered in the alleyway. Juniper stood, ready to flee, just as a young man appeared, holding a little metal tray containing four glasses of hot milk-tea.

"Welcome, madam, to my shop! You like some chai?"

Juniper breathed deep and sat down on the stool. "Sure. I would love a chai, thank you," she said. She gestured around the shop as though she'd just arrived.

"You have some beautiful stonework here," she said. "But tell me. Where do you keep your statues of Kali?"

CROWN

"Give to such a woman the knowledge of the forms
and customs of society, teach her how best to show the gentle
courtesies of life, and you have a lady, created by God, only
indebted for the outward polish to the world."

The Ladies' Book of Etiquette, and Manual of Politeness, 1860

RE: DIVISION UNIFICATION

Golden Poultry Processing Plant
MEMO
To: All Golden Poultry division employees
From: Kitty Ingram Lanford
RE: Division Unification

As you know, Boss Karpinski likes to say that we here at Golden Poultry should all aim for division unification. Better workers, he says, produce better teams; better teams make for better projects; better projects create a better office atmosphere, which brings better leadership, all of which contributes to a better, more unified division, which, in turn, makes our company succeed. The company is considered successful when it makes more money. And it is the division's office's leader's team's project's members—each of us—who are charged with making that happen.

To motivate us into further unifying our division, Karpinski tells us to get our "ducks in a row," to "think outside the box," and to always leave "room on our plate." Achieving these three goals, he says, will no doubt put "a feather in our cap."

More than once, he has noted that members of our division's team must "wear many hats" in order to succeed. This in particular caught my attention because I have yet to see anyone in our division, save for myself, wear a single hat, let alone several. I did a good stretch of knitting a few years back, after my father died and before my daughter joined the Marching Tigers, and those of you who work on my team in our division's office know that I actually own and wear an extensive collection of woolen hats—although not at the same time. I'd like to know why Boss Karpinski suggests that we all wear hats, then, when in fact I am the division's sole multiple hat wearer. I can imagine he'll read this memo and say, "there's no 'I' in 'team,' Kitty Ingram." But there's no 'we' in team, either. Only "me," mixed up. And wearing all the hats. And while I see boxes of chocolates and boxed pens doled to my colleagues as quarterly rewards, I—the lone multi-hat wearer of our division—have yet to see a reward, let alone a single feather, for my cap—or caps, as it were—come my way.

Perhaps the source of these elusive feathers is the ducks which Mr. Karpinski is so fond of aligning. Every time he urges us to get our "ducks in a row," I can't help but think we are getting bad advice. My father was a prize duck hunter out at Mattamuskeet each year, Mallard Class, and I know that, unless they are stuffed and mounted on your mantle, ducks do not readily get in rows, nor do they like to. As everyone knows, ducks in flight make v-shaped formations, which is not a row but rather an elegant, egalitarian arc. And anyone who's ever watched ducks in a marsh could tell you they aren't about to line up for you when they're sitting in the water. That's why they make buckshot. Yet Mr. Karpinski seems to believe that there is some relationship between row-friendly ducks and our mission of division unification. But to put them in rows is contrary not only to the natural tendencies of ducks, but also to the true aim of the statement, by which I assume he means: get organized.

But in order to get organized, he wants us to think outside the very object that would help us, logistically, to achieve it. It has been nearly three decades since I have been able to maneuver my body to fit inside a box, let alone think inside of one. And, unless you are compelled to place a box over your head as inspiration to get the neurons firing, thinking outside of a box is a natural, if not logical, thing to do. It begs the question why a box would even need to be present in order for thought to occur. My experience suggests that thinking happens—and should happen—when no box is present. So it makes one wonder: why the emphasis on the box? If, perhaps, the word "box" is meant to suggest my rather boxlike "cubicle," then I heartily agree. And, since boxes tend to stay where you put them—except if that box happens to be in the supply room closet filled with staples and designer pushpins and the four-dollars-a-pop fountain pens and deluxe desk calendar—it seems a far simpler and more logical task to put your boxes in a row, and to let the ducks outside where they belong.

By solving the dilemmas of box placement and duck-alignment, it frees us, then, to consider Mr. Karpinski's third piece of advice to achieve division unification. When I first heard him say, "don't tell me your plate is full; always leave a little room," I thought he was talking about the holiday all-you-can-eat chicken buffet the division pays for down in the break room. It's advice I get from my dietician, too. And my therapist. But I always want to know, and no one ever tells me: what are we leaving room on our plates for? Ducks? In boxes? But then I realized that leaving room on a plate simply means that there is more to life than ducks and boxes and Golden Poultry, for that matter, and that you need to be ready for it. Leaving room on your plate is, in essence, making room for change, something that would mix up and rehash stale leftovers, be it food or phrase. Maybe it's something that might inspire you to leave the division's office for a while, even for just an hour, to take a walk in the woods to experience box-free thinking. And maybe you'd find in the woods a lake, where, if you are lucky enough, you may come across a family of ducks and observe them. You would know how unwilling they'd be to get in rows for you, how easily they spook if you rush at them, scare them a little into taking flight. I used to do this when I was a girl, on those Saturday mornings duck hunting with my dad. I'd rush at the ducks and when they flew away, a feather sometimes would fall from their fold, and land, miraculously, at my feet.

MARCHERS

I KNEW THE FIRST TIME I SAW HIM MARCHING among the other children, this would be the first of a decade's worth of parades I'd sit through, cheering, waving, catching float candy for later. Turns out I was right. In the past twelve years, Toby moved from Cub Scouts to Soccer to marching band, and now here he is, Mr. Drum Major of the Mewborn High School Marching Tigers, keeping his classmates lockstep in maroon polyester, proud and strong, arm pumping the pole, leading the way down Main Street.

Contrary to what you might think, halftime entertainment for the footballers is just a sliver of what the Marching Tigers do. These kids play for veterans. They play for charity carwashes and pancake suppers. They play for homecoming parades and Thanksgiving games and every regional celebration in between. They play today, in the heat of July, because we are American. At competition time, they dominate in Raleigh, saving for the grandstand judges at the homestretch their prize-winning "Louie Louie" grooves pitched to a Sousa stride. But they need no prize to play their hearts out. And I never once had to tell Toby the reward is in a job well done. You can hear it now, in each drumbeat, in every hand-blown note.

Today the Marching Tigers' melody energizes the armies of tall-booted baton twirlers and troupes of sturdy Girl Scouts, their green sashes heavy with hand-sewn badges; it thrums for the candy-tossing Ruritans and Future Farmers of America who hang their hand-stitched flags amid the massive crop dioramas on their flatbed trucks. Giant foam cob corn and squash and such. It envelops the Watermelon and Shad Queens and all the other harvest prize beauties who, until this year, usually sit hip to hip in convertibles with the Homecoming Court. You should see these girls in their gauze and tulle, lovely lipstick smiles and long gloves at ten in the morning, sitting up in the backseats of the handful of sportscars Kitty Ingram Lanford usually secures during parade season. For years our Marching Tigers Booster Club's Civic Parade Committee was lush with drivers, thanks to her meticulous list. She's a powerhouse at home games, prospecting the old coots, leaving hand-scrawled notes on windshields of convertibles in the parking lots of the Noontime Rotary and Kiwanis meeting halls. It's harder than you think to find a civic-minded man with enough cash to afford a third car payment but who doesn't slip away on the weekends to a boat down in Little Washington or some second home on the Crystal Coast. And after what happened this spring with Lars Stokes and the Shad Queen, it's even harder. Our drivers have dwindled to nearly half. I probably don't have to explain what might have happened for you to catch on, but I'll leave it at this: girl gone bad, or wild, or whatever. And as embarrassing as it is for their families, I can't begin to tell what a mess it's been for everyone else. Last week Kitty Ingram called me in tears, nearly, blaming everything on poor Lars.

"To steal a phrase from our friends in Homeland Security, We are Code Red on the convertible front," she said. "And it's not the men who won't drive these girls; it's their wives who won't let them: 'the next Sissy Saunders in every back seat,' one told me.'" That's why today there's five girls to a car instead of three, and why the Cotton and Collard Queens ride with the Ruritans instead of with the Misses Tight End and Wide Receiver of the Homecoming Court. "It's not fair to divide up the ag queens from football gals," Kitty Ingram said this morning, clipboard in hand, "but I don't know what else to do."

Let Kitty Ingram say what she will. Out here on Main Street, the parade looks fantastic. Armies of kids pass with their "Rockets and Whistles" themed wagons and bicycles. Pickup trucks stuffed with hay bales hold the handful of veterans who still fit in their dress uniforms. The men manage to salute for nearly the entire route, too old to walk the half-mile, too dignified to toss candy. Teams of Shriners zoom by in fezzes and funny cars. Unless you're looking for a particular princess, you really don't notice which frosting-clad beauty sits where. You don't notice that Lars Stokes's cherry red 1965 Corvair Monza is gone from the queue, or that Sissy Saunders, the should-have-been Shad Queen, is missing and the runner-up is waving in her place. Lovely as those girls are, after a while they all start to look alike—but what do I know? In high school, my sisters and I were all big on field hockey, not beauty contests. But try telling that to Kitty Ingram Lanford, a former beauty queen herself.

And try telling that to Lars Stokes, who, by all accounts, had responded to Sissy as any unthinking man might. I guess if I had a daughter, I'd feel different—but I still say it's a shame what happened, and not just because Mary lost a reliable driver or that Lars's life is ruined on account of a few kisses with some tiara-twit teenage carrot-top. None of that is really my business. But what is my business is how far downhill the Marching Tigers' monthly pancake suppers has gone since the incident. Lars' daughter had played tenor sax, and after his wife left him—the same year Toby joined the Junior Marching Tigers—Lars got involved with the Boosters. He'd tinkered up a bicycle-powered, rotating griddle for the Booster's monthly pancake fundraiser dinner, said it was something he'd always had the mind to do. I'll never forget the first time he came to the high school with his contraption in tow. The griddle is the size of a kitchen table, made of nonstick aluminum, that attaches to a crank Lars hooked up to the pedal part of a bicycle. At the right temperature, that griddle bike can cook sixty fail-free pancakes in a single rotation. At three cakes each, that's twenty people fed in seven minutes, and after WITN ran a feature, folks as far as Tarboro and Creswell used to drive out just to see the Marching Tigers Booster Club's griddle bike pancake maker. At first, all the Booster moms—myself included—asked Lars to run the bicycle: imagine losing weight while making pancakes! But Lars would never let any of us near it, said it was a liability. Later we fought—out of his earshot—who'd get to flip the cakes, on account of the buns-level view the back of the bike afforded. Each month we packed in hundreds of pancake eaters, and at seven dollars a plate, you do the math. Our coffers were fat. The new uniforms were beautiful, and each band member got a $300 subsidy for their trip to the Nationals.

And all was well until this spring, just before Shad Daze, when the Shad Queen went and ruined everything. Like I said, no one knows exactly what happened, because Sissy is underage and the paper wouldn't run the real-real story. All that ran was that Lars was arrested for "unlawful conduct with a minor" and he posted a cash bail bond of five thousand dollars. And even Toby tells me that the one who'd started it—whatever it was that got started—was the Shad Queen herself, that it was her mother who caught them smooching in his Corvair after the parade, and it was her mother who called the cops. Lars pled guilty, and to stay out of jail agreed to stay away from all events involving children. Unfortunately for us, this includes the pancake suppers and all the parades and ballgames. As Kitty Ingram says, "There goes our prize Corvair." And I say, there goes the Marching Tigers Booster Club's Cash Cow Pancake Griddle Bicycle. And even with her title stripped, Toby tells me our little Miss Vixen Shad Queen is off, scot-free, a full ride to State in the fall.

No one thinks about the fate of parades or pancakes or the Marching Tigers Booster Club when she comes on to a man her daddy's age. And no one thinks about the consequences—let alone the stupidity—of responding to the advances of a child two months shy of being a legal adult. Ever since Lars and his griddle bike were banned from school property, our pancake suppers are chaos. It's no picnic lugging around one of nine fry pan hibachis and mini-propane fuel packs.

And the inconsistency in product that comes with the presence of nine cooks, each of whom thinks she is running the show, is downright embarrassing. I bow out of the catfight among the Booster moms. I just smile down at my own pancakes, ready with my spatula, counting the days until this is over. Of course, I don't go around advertising that when Toby's gone and graduated, so am I. No more pancakes for me. No more parades. Heaven forbid I end up like Kitty Ingram, who should have retired from all this three years ago, when her daughter graduated. And we know what happened to Lars, who was probably lonely after his divorce and wanted to make some new friends with his griddle bike. There are costs to everything we do. Sad as I am to see Toby grow up and get off to college, I'm glad there's an end to all of this, and I'm especially glad that I'm heading out on the coattails of the golden era of the Lars Stokes griddle bike. Our supper customers talk with longing about the "old-school" pancakes, which says without saying that the ones we make now aren't worth the seven dollars. And our coffers show that, ever since Lars' arrest, our pancake profits dipped. As Kitty Ingram says, "We've got that Hussy Shad Queen to thank for it." Kitty Ingram sometimes calls Lars, pretending like nothing terrible happened, to ask if he'd lend or rent out his griddle bike. Or she'll get me to call so she doesn't appear too pesky. It's awkward asking, and every time he refuses. "I've done enough, and I've had enough, Catherine," he'll say, and I can hear the sadness in his voice and I tell him I understand so he won't feel so alone. And even though I don't say this to Kitty Ingram, I cannot blame him.

Still, it's amazing the things we do for our children: asking the town's alleged pervert for his pancake maker. Or standing on the side of the road, camera in hand, waiting to take the perfect shot. Sure, I'd rather be on my couch with a book, or crocheting afghans for the church fair. And while my sister Becky tells me that I could easily find another man to keep me company—and for full disclosure I'll admit that until recently Lars had been on her short list—I keep to myself ever since Toby's daddy died. Toby was just four; old enough to know his daddy was gone but too young to understand a heart attack. Thank God Toby and I still have each other.

And now here he comes, leading the thrumming pack of drummers, the kids holding the horns and the xylos, hoping to God the horses keep their sphincters in check. Rule is, you march right through, no matter what. And Toby looks great. He's earned this moment—at the center of the entire parade, keeping pace with his baton for all the little ones in the back. He's so intent on keeping time he fails to catch my eye as he passes by, even though I yell his name when I click the shutter. The wave of drums rattles and surges and then it's over. In the fall he's off to college, and all this pancake and parade business, Kitty Ingram and Lars, will be a thing of the past. I rise up on tiptoe and lift the camera above my head, in Toby's direction, hoping the frame will capture this last glimpse of him, the back of his high stiff hat, and the marchers who follow in his wake.

SHAD DAZE

NOAH WAS NEARLY NAKED IN AN INNER TUBE, telling Wendy about his family.

Ma's got round glasses. Dark ringlets like his, cropped short.

Dad's a walking refrigerator. Cheeks made of ham.

"Sissy looks a lot like dad, but meaner," Noah said. "Can't miss her."

"Oh, come on," Wendy said. "She can't be that mean."

"You'll see," he said.

Noah and Wendy floated down the Neuse River in their underwear, bottoms and bellies sunk in the liquid O centers of giant rubber donuts. Arms and legs dangled over the edge. Cinched with string to the tubes were the clothes they wore into town, all the way from Philadelphia, waterproofed in triple-wrapped plastic bags.

Noah arched his back to dip the crown of his head in the stream. The water was warm for an April afternoon in North Carolina. He'd insisted they leave that morning at five to spend the afternoon in the Neuse before he introduced Wendy to the reality of his family: Granny supposedly on her deathbed; Sissy about as mean as they make them; Ma and Dad, as ever, docile and oblivious.

He shouldn't have been surprised that the river trip brought back memories of his best friend, Knox. It had been only two years since they took his ashes to Porter Bridge, and Noah hadn't returned since. Knox would have liked to see Noah here with Wendy. Finally, he'd say. You grew a pair and got out here without me. Knox would appreciate, as Noah did now, how Wendy crossed her legs over the curve of the inner tube, how her long fingertips skimmed the surface of the Neuse, how her thin cotton bra showed, in its dampness, the precise scope and curve of her breasts.

"What are you thinking about?" Wendy asked. "Your grandmother?"

"No. Thinking about you. Thinking about the last time I was out here," he said.

"When was that?"

"With my buddy, Knox. Just before I left for school. That kid loved to smoke. Everywhere we went he smoked, even out on the river."

"So much for being one with nature," Wendy said.

"No kidding," Noah said. "I'll never forget, this one time we were cruising on the water, and he's all excited, telling this joke about a pet whisperer, or something, when the tip of his cigarette burns a hole in the tube, and the thing starts deflating. Nearly sunk with him still on it. He rode down the river on his belly, holding onto my tube. And the guy up at the gas station charged him ten bucks to patch it."

"Is Knox still in town?"

He knew she'd ask. "No," Noah said. "He's not." He splashed in Wendy's direction. "There's Porter Bridge. Let's kick to shore."

They slipped their bodies through the inner tubes' holes and kicked crosscut of the current to the rocky lip of the river, then climbed up the steep slope to the roadway, where they'd chained their bikes to a streetlight. Wendy untied the plastic bags that held their clothes and flip-flops, and they dressed on the gravel shoulder of the road.

Noah paused from dressing for a moment to look at Wendy, whose wet underwear showed the line that divided the moon of her butt. Her legs were long, shoulders almost too narrow for the heft of her breasts, the girlish girth of her hips.

"Now that's a nice, free show," Noah said.

"It's not a show if there's no audience," Wendy said, slipping a shirt over her still-wet bra, darkening her yellow tank top in triangular patches. She patted her dark hair with her towel. "I can see you, too."

"I wonder what my folks will say when they meet you," he said. He reached for her hand, pulling her toward him. Her skin was cool, alive. Perfect. "They'll be so surprised."

"You told them you were bringing me, right?"

"Not exactly," he said. "No."

"Noah," Wendy said. She pulled back from him. "What the hell?"

"What?" he asked.

"Are you keeping me a secret?" she asked. She unlocked the bicycles.

"There's no secrets," he said. He hid the tubes under the bridge; he'd come by for them later with the car. "Just surprises. I don't talk to my family much. You ready?"

They got on their bicycles and began the two-mile ride toward the gas station, where Noah had left the car.

"So, tell me about this Knox guy," Wendy said, as they rode along the quiet highway. Noah couldn't answer her just then. But soon they'd be away from the Neuse. Soon they could get in his car and go anywhere, and he could tell Wendy anything she wanted. But riding so close to the river, he felt too close to him, to all of it.

"Knox was just… a friend," Noah said. He could feel the creak and groan of his bike pedals. "But he's not here anymore."

EXCEPT FOR THE DRIVEWAY, which was empty, everything at the Saunders's looked the same as Noah remembered. Noah's folks lived in an older house in a newish development where all the homes looked more or less the same: a brick façade, a thin front porch, islands of pine straw with requisite shrubs, and a gazing globe that failed to ever tell anyone's fortune.

"I was kind of expecting a big welcome," Noah said, as he found the house key. "Mom's wanted me home for months." Noah's "hello" echoed through the house, unanswered. The first floor was tidy but held the smell of an unflushed toilet.

"Granny's got to be in there," Noah said, gesturing to the closed door off the dining room. "This here's her wheelchair."

"Shouldn't you check on her?" Wendy asked.

"I don't want to complicate things," he said. "She confuses easily."

In the kitchen was a plate of plastic-wrapped, fish-shaped cookies and a note from Mom: "Dear Noah, We are down at the Shad Festival. Clara Martin is ill and I have to run the SHAD-O til one. Please come find us for dinner. Sissy will come for Granny at three for dialysis. Love, Mom."

"Guess we know what's for supper," Noah said.

"Shad?" Wendy asked. "Like, little fish?"

"You got it," Noah said. He'd eaten the herring on their seasonal upstream runs on the Neuse since he was a boy. Knox's dad had even taken them fishing a time or two, but they never caught any. They'd just stand in the river, poles in hand as Mr. Karpinski pounded Pabst and the shad moved past, un-tempted by their shiny lures.

Noah took a bite of the shortbread shad cookie. "Let me show you around."

Noah showed Wendy the screened-in sun room with the daybed where his folks would probably make him sleep. The adjacent den held a massive television, a shag rug, and a mantle full of mounted fish. On the wall of the stairwell to the second floor were dozens of family photos: Sissy in her knockout days was rail-thin and red-haired, her smile saucy and come-hither in the photo, even in her sparkling celery colored dress and Shad Queen tiara. Dad had taken that shot just before Knox and Sissy got together. When Mom called Noah at school to tell him about Knox and Sissy dating, he was glad to hear it. Noah had dated Knox's sister Colleen, off and on, although nothing really came of it. But Noah had always hoped Sissy and Knox would have worked it out. If they got married, he liked to joke with Knox, he'd have his best friend for a brother-in-law. And then he'd heard

Sissy had been getting in neck-deep with all the party kids up at the college during her senior year of high school. And after that whole thing with the Pancake Man, she decided to ditch college altogether, and she decided to take Knox with her. He'd warned Knox, and Sissy, too, that she'd probably get them both in trouble. And then she did.

"So this is her, huh?" Wendy said.

"Not anymore," Noah said. "Sissy's…different now."

"Do you miss her? How she was?"

"It's hard to know what I miss about her," he said. "But I do." Next to Sissy's Shad Queen shot was Noah and Knox at their high school graduation, Sissy wedged between them. Their parents posing at the beach, squinting eyes, smiling into the sun.

"Fucking Sissy," Noah mumbled.

"Why are you so angry?" Wendy asked.

"Wait'll you meet Sissy. Then you'll see who's angry," Noah said. He climbed the rest of the stairs.

"Maybe she just needs someone to understand her," Wendy said. She lingered at the wall of photos. "It's all so sad."

"If you want sad," Noah said, walking down the hall to his childhood bedroom, "come see where you'll sleep tonight." It had been more than fifteen years since Noah's mother decorated him a room inspired by Batman—complete with a bat-shaped headboard, a dozen bat mobiles, and hand-stenciled bat walls. It still made him cringe.

"Hand-made by Mom," he said. "I must have been four."

"Wow. So did you have a thing for Batman?" Wendy asked.

Noah shrugged. "Can't remember."

"Why hasn't she changed it into a guest room?" Wendy asked. "Or something less…batty?"

"Probably waiting to be discovered by *Better Homes* or something," He swatted at the mobile of bat-shaped silhouettes that hung from a Bat-shaped light fixture.

"Or for you to move home," she said. "Mama's boy."

"That won't happen," he said.

Each bat was hand-stenciled in gold and metallic blue on navy walls. The mobile bats were cut and sanded smooth, painted the same shade as the walls. A flannel, hand-stitched bat silhouette spread its golden wings across the navy bedspread quilt.

"Why don't you ask her to redecorate?" Wendy asked.

"I never had the heart to tell Mom all these bats kind of creep me out," Noah said. He felt around under the back of Wendy's shirt for her bra clasp. They moved toward the bed. "You see, all this? It's not really Batman," he said, pushing up her shirt. "It's just bats. A thousand bats. I counted once."

"Noah, your grandmother," she breathed into his ear, moving in closer to his body, reaching for the fly of his shorts.

"She can't hear a thing," he said. He slid his hands under her skirt. "As deaf as they make 'em. You'll see when you meet her."

"This whole Granny deathbed business, is it going to be okay with me here?" Wendy asked.

Noah played with a lock of Wendy's hair. "Mom called me about it last month, and Granny isn't gone yet," Noah said. "Besides, no one really likes Granny anyway. I mean, we love her and all. But before she lost her mind, she was one of the meanest nurses you ever met."

EVEN WITH ALL HE'D TOLD HER ABOUT SISSY THAT AFTERNOON, Noah was surprised Wendy was still determined to befriend her, to try to tap into, as Wendy said, "what made her real." So it didn't seem fair, then, that Sissy's first view of Wendy was of her panting naked on the hand-sewn Batman bedspread, legs spread, with Noah kneeling between them.

There was no denying that Sissy had launched a stealth attack, climbing the stairs undetected, as only she knew how, and then standing silent in the doorway. At some point, Noah had felt Wendy stiffen, and then gasp aloud and not in a good way. He could only imagine that, past the dangling bat mobiles, Wendy was staring at his sister smirking in the hallway. Before Noah could react, Wendy shrieked, shielding her breasts with her arms. She kicked Noah in the eye with her heel before folding herself into a ball on the bed. Noah clutched his eye, now throbbing.

"What the fuck, Sissy?" he said. No one said anything for a moment, and just as Noah opened his mouth, Sissy said, "They got all the fish you want, Noah, down at the festival." Her footfalls on the stairwell were as quiet going down as they were coming up. "And may God in heaven forget to save your wretched, cussing, sinning souls," she said.

"Go to hell yourself, Sissy," Noah yelled, helpless, as Wendy reached for her underwear. His eye was well on its way to bruising.

"Are you okay?" Wendy asked.

"That was Sissy," Noah said. He stood, pressing his palm into his eye, wanting ice. He swatted at the bat mobile with his other hand. "Still think you can win her over?"

Every spring, Noah told Wendy, as they drove to the field behind Mewborn High School, the entire town shakes with river shad. It's boiled and shredded into fried cakes, hacked into stew, grilled in small slabs, breaded with cornmeal and deep-fried whole like chicken, eyes and all, in hot grease. They are tossed, frozen, as sport. Caught in batches and mounted in taxidermy workshops. People in hand-made fish costumes shake fins with visitors, meandering through the festival, posing for photographs like Mickey Mouse.

"I wonder how the fish feels," Wendy said, as they entered the festival. "It's like, all these people are saying: we love you because we eat you. Or: we eat you because we love you."

"Not much else here to do but get your fish freak on," Noah said.

"Maybe you can win me a stuffed fish?" she asked.

"I already have one," he said. "You can have it."

"Wait," Wendy said. "T-shirts!"

At the Shad Shirt booth, people slathered the little fish in paint, then pressed them in custom patterns against T-shirts. Noah had donned his classic "SHAD DAZED AND CONFUZED" T-shirt for the occasion. It was the very one that got Wendy and Noah talking down at the Philly flea market the first day they met, about a year ago, sorting through a stack of dollar bin vinyl records. Wendy told him later she'd noticed the imprints of scales across his shirt and got the courage to ask him when was the last time he'd hugged a fish. And he'd wrapped his arms around himself and said, "I'm my own favorite Pisces, thank you." When she said she was a Pisces, too, he hugged her.

"I definitely need a fish Tee," Wendy said. "You know, to come full circle."

"You just don't want anyone to think you're a Shad Fest virgin."

"Well, I guess it's good to still be a virgin of something," she said. And they laughed, embarrassed, when a stout woman in a spun-white bouffant turned around and glared at them. "Let's just get these T-shirts underway," Noah said.

Wendy took a bottle of blue puffy paint and a fish patted dry with a paper towel. Roller paint at the ready, she spread out the T-shirts. On the front of one shirt, she wrote, "I ♥ a Guy who ♥'s to Eat Shad!" with a left-pointed arrow. On the back, she wrote "It's Shad-alingus!!" On Noah's T-shirt she wrote, "I'm the Guy who ♥'s to Eat Shad!" with an arrow pointing up.

"Why taunt her?" Noah said.

"Sissy needs to know we aren't afraid of her," Wendy said. "We eat fish and we like it!"

"It's a bad idea around here," Noah said, "to turn shad into a joke about oral sex."

"It could have been worse," Wendy said. "It could have been your mom who found us."

"We'd have heard Mom long before she ever got up the stairs," he said.

"Do you think Sissy will say anything?"

"What's she gonna say?" Noah said.

"Something like: 'That Wendy girl is trash.' Just one little thing speaks volumes, you know?"

"Or she'll just hold it over our heads," Noah said. "Sibling blackmail gets my vote."

"It's bad enough getting caught, but what gets me is that she didn't look away," Wendy said. "Clear her throat. Something. She had to have seen your car in the yard. Who knows how long she'd been there, fingering that gold cross around her neck?"

"I don't know," Noah said.

"I mean, she was prowling around. We caught her catching us," she said. Wendy pounded the fish into the back of the T-shirt. "In my book?" she said, "voyeurism's the real sin."

"Careful," Noah said. "The idea is to imprint the fish on the shirt, not pummel it."

The fish was now quite flat. "Sorry," Wendy said.

"Say it to the fish, not me," Noah said.

When she was finished, Wendy gave the woman at the checkout twenty dollars and the two shirts. Behind her were a dozen shirts on a clothesline, quick-drying in the breeze of a giant floor fan.

"Come back for them in ten, hon," the woman said. She began to write down the T-shirt slogans on a long list with her chewed-up ballpoint.

"We're always looking for the next Shad Daze slogan," she said. "Usually the best ones come from this booth."

She paused before she made an ellipsis after the "I ♥ a guy who…" Then she looked at Noah and said, "Well, ain't you Bif Saunders's boy? Noah?"

"Yes, ma'am," Noah said. "Ms. Martin?"

"You got that right. Free Will misses you! We haven't seen you for a good couple years," she said.

"I been up north at school," he said.

"Good for you," Ms. Martin said. "Your hair got long."

"Yes ma'am," Noah said. He gestured to Wendy. "This is my…"

"What happened to your eye?"

"An accident, ma'am," he said.

"You hear Colleen Karpinski is dancing tonight?"

Noah glanced at Wendy and said, "No, ma'am. Haven't seen a program." Ms. Martin frowned as she handed him a stapled booklet with a pair of cartoon Shad wearing sunglasses and playing saxophones.

"Take mine," she said. "I have two. That girl's a real star, that Colleen. Shame about her brother."

"Yes, ma'am," Noah said. He found the schedule. Colleen Karpinski, he learned, was not only dancing that night, but she and three other former Shad Queens were co-hosting the pageant for the next crop of satin-clad beauties. Her photo was stunning. The slight bump on her nose made her wide-set eyes, her broad smile and shining dark hair, all the more compelling. She looked like Knox.

"Who is Colleen?" Wendy asked.

"No one," Noah said, too quickly. He felt a prickle of jealousy in Wendy's question. "Used to be friends with Sissy." He closed the booklet and said to the woman, "Thank you for this. I think we'll take those shirts now. We got to go find my folks. Oh, and this is Wendy." The woman cast a wary look at Wendy, all teeth.

"Charmed," she said. Then, to Noah: "You take care of that eye."

Noah and Wendy held hands, cutting through the snaking line of people to get under a white, circus-sized tent with purple crosses painted on the roof. On stage, a lone man with a guitar sang a song about waterways.

"Where'd they get such a huge tent?" Wendy asked. "With such huge crosses?"

"A loan from the Revivalists," Noah said. "They have their big camp meeting the week before the Shad festival, and to keep the permit people in town happy, they leave it up for the Shad folks."

Seas of people were eating fish at red picnic tables aligned in long rows.

"How will we find your folks?" Wendy asked.

"They sit in the same section every year," he said. "Like panning for gold. You stake your claim once and it's yours."

They found Noah's dad in the center row, reading the newspaper.

"Hope you like shad," Dad said to Wendy when Noah introduced them. "That's what's on the menu."

"Where's Ma?" Noah asked.

"She left to meet Sissy and take Granny to dialysis," Dad said. "They should be here soon."

"I'm getting hungry."

Dad nodded toward the parking lot.

"Here they come now," he said. They followed his gaze. Sissy was pushing an elderly woman with bright pink hair.

"What the hell has Granny got on her head?" Noah asked.

"Sissy brought home one of them fuchsia bobs at Halloween? One of them ten-buck rat's nests you can find over in Wilson? And damned if that's the one thing Mother remembers when she leaves the house," Dad said. "She forgets her own name but won't be seen without that wig."

Ma went straight to the pre-order express food line. Sissy found the family picnic table as though there were a painted line leading her to it. She didn't say hello to anyone, and made a show of locking the wheels on Granny's chair. She started in complaining about the trouble she'd had with Granny's catheter, how long the dialysis line was today.

"I don't see why they don't have one line for all the junkies, and one for the normal people who just need to get their kidneys clean," she said.

"That's what we need in this world," Noah said. "Even more privileged health care, based on your moral past."

"The trash they let in that place," Dad said, in a humoring tone.

"Course you can find trash in your own home, too." Sissy said, staring at Wendy. "If your timing's right."

"Watch it, Sissy," said Noah. He leaned toward Granny and shouted, "Isn't your hair the prettiest shade of pink!" And Granny patted Noah's hand and smiled. "You like my hair?" she said. Noah nodded.

"Sis, you meet Wendy here?" Dad said. "Noah's friend from school."

"Charmed," Sissy said. Her gaze tracked the food line. "Ima go help Ma now with dinner. Like I do everything else around here."

"Take your time, Sis," Noah called after her. "Nice to see you, too."

"Hey, Colleen is on the bill tonight," Dad said. "That gal's a heck of a stepper." Noah turned to his father.

"How's Granny been?" he asked. "Really."

"About the same," he said. "Not much changes around here. You know that."

"Sissy's still on her Red Banks kick?"

"Well…" Dad said. He shrugged. "We manage. She's talking about doing a health aide program, but who knows what'll come of it."

"I hear there's a need for nursing assistants nationwide," said Wendy. "Wasn't Mrs. Saunders a nurse?"

"Nurse!" Noah yelled at his grandmother. He pointed to her in a You-you-you gesture. She nodded. "Some forty years," she said.

Sissy and Mom returned from the shad line with two trays each filled with deep-fried baby shad fish, cartons of collards and beans, and rolls so slathered with brushed butter they shone.

"I been waiting on this all year," Dad said.

Mom set down the trays and pulled Noah to standing to give him a hug. "You didn't tell us you had a girlfriend," she said. She kept her arms wrapped around him as she gave Wendy the once-over. "Noah doesn't tell us much, but usually he'll mention the important stuff. Like how he got a bruised eye. Now, what happened?"

"Nice to meet you," Wendy said. "We had a little accident this afternoon."

"I'm all right, Ma," he said. "We were..."

"We were down at the river," Wendy said. "Enjoying the day."

"That's not all you been enjoying," Sissy said. Granny shifted in her chair and reached for one of the fried fish. Sissy slapped Granny on the wrist and shook her head. Granny dropped the fish like a thief, caught.

"Let her be, Sis," Noah said. "She's not a child."

"Don't you tell me what to do," Sissy said. "We got to give a grace first." She bent low to Granny and yelled, "Grace!"

"I guess that's a sign it's time we eat," Dad said. Sissy took Granny's greasy hand, then her mother's, then dropped her head. Sissy prayed for the health of her family and friends, the tastiness of the shad of which they were about to eat, and that the souls of all sinners would seek to be saved so that they may find a place in the Kingdom of the Lord on Judgment Day. "And may those sinners, Lord, who fail to repent their ways, be forever scarred by your wrath, until they find it in their hearts to seek your forgiveness," Sissy said. "Amen."

"Holy Bullshit," Noah muttered, as everyone but Wendy lifted their heads and grabbed a shad. They held the fish like an ear of corn, and bit in. Granny picked up the fish and licked her lips, smiled at it as though it were an old friend. She pushed aside some hot pink strands of hair stuck to her lip, then downed it in three precise bites. Dad brought his own seasoning—Mrs. Dash—on account of his high blood pressure. "Gotta cut back on the salt," he said. He eyed Sissy. "You should, too, sweetie."

"Keep that shaker away from my fish. You know I don't like spicy," she said. Her nose scrunched up, making her cheeks puff out, her mouth full of food. Sissy was already on her third shad. "The Lord will provide."

"Looks like he's provided enough already," Noah said. He ignored Wendy's thump on his arm.

Sissy ignored him as she buttered her buttered roll. Ma managed to avoid any talk about things that mattered: Granny's health, the presence of his girlfriend. She added to the din of the crowd as they ate, telling Noah news about who got married, who had a baby, who joined the Army, who sold his car, who got a new one.

The table was quiet as the Mewborn High School Show Choir waved aquatic-colored sashes for their "Under the Sea" routine. Noah had planned to tell his family how Wendy grew up in Connecticut, how she could add huge sums in her head. That she spent last summer building elementary schools in Peru. How they might go back there together this summer. But he couldn't shake Sissy's sneery "fish eating" comment from that afternoon, how she crept up the stairs to spy on him and had ruined Wendy's chances with his folks. All of this had lodged into him and refused to leave the little place inside where he held grudges. He watched Sissy get grease and cornmeal stuck to her chin as she ate, and thought back to all the times he and Knox had come here, sitting at this very table, downing the ancestors of these same fish. One year Knox had switched out the Red Banks Church's praise choir's "He is the Fount of Love" cassette with "Rebel Yell." They were sitting right there when all the lace-collar control freak church ladies screeched at the sound man to "turn off that devil music."

Noah found himself staring at Sissy as she ate, unable to look away from her seemingly opaque stay-at-home grown child's eyes, unforgiving and cold. He wanted to ask Sissy why she chose to make everyone around her miserable. And who the hell did she think she was, bringing Knox down like she did?

But then Wendy sighed, and put down her fork.

"I can't do this," she said.

"What's the matter?" Sissy asked. "Can't eat fish?"

Ma gnawed on a roll from the basket, her eyes fixed on the stage as though it were a television screen. "Oh, Noah, almost forgot. You know, Colleen is dancing tonight."

"Heard all about it," Noah said.

"That trash," Sissy said. "You figure the organizers would be smart enough than to pick her. When I was…"

"Sis, now wait, you are heaps trashier than Colleen could ever be," Noah said. "And everyone knows it. Don't get all high and mighty now because you think God's on your side."

"Don't you take the lord's name in vain to me," Sissy said.

Wendy shook her head at her uneaten food. "I can't do this," she said.

"Well, Sissy. Why do you suppose they didn't they ask you to co-host the competition this year with all the other former Shad Queens?" he said.

"You need to mind your own," Sissy said. "I wouldn't have done it if they asked."

"If they're smart, they never will," Noah said. He grabbed Wendy by the shoulder, leaned into her as though he was going to tell her a secret. "Wendy, check it out. You want to know what trash is? I'll tell you. It wasn't a half-hour after they crowned her Shad Queen that Sissy here changed into her skintight jeans and some skank top and proceeded to get soused down at the carnival," Noah said.

Wendy shrunk away from his hand on her shoulder. "Noah, I don't think…"

"And so there she was, our fair fish lady, in her roadhouse clothes and tiara and sash, with this gauzy cape wrap thing they put around your shoulders to make it look like you been blessed by a fish or something. And it took but an hour for Sissy here to down a bottle of

Peachtree on the fairway, and then toss it all up on the Spider Ride."

Noah hardly heard his mother ask to keep his voice down. He focused on the pair of women on stage singing, "Let the River Run." Their hair was electric-socket big, over-permed and tamed by AquaNet.

"You shoulda seen it—the whole crowd, covered in Miss Shad Priss's Peachtree-shad puke, and the operator didn't notice, 'cause he was talking to some gal. Even though people are, like, screaming at him to stop the ride," Noah said.

Noah raised his voice as though he was telling the story to the women on stage.

"And by the time she was done, Sis and her pals were covered in fish vomit and they had to wrap a big plastic bag around her spider seat for the rest of the carnival."

"Shut up, will you?" Sissy said, standing up. Her face was contorted and red. "Just shut up."

"So what does Sissy do? Strips down to her skivvies right there on the railroad tracks, then tries to walk around in nothing but that cape and her undies and her sparkly purse. Oh, and the Shad sash and tiara, too. Knox and me had to corral her like we was border collies, just to get her home. And the next year, they had to get a new cape for all Sissy had done to it. And then there was the thing with the Pancake dude…"

When the collards, rolls and whatever else was on the tray between Noah and his sister landed on him, even he knew he deserved it. Sissy heaved a rather loud "Go to hell" at Noah before she pushed her way through the crowd. Ma followed, casting back at Noah an awful glare. He'd gone too far. But he couldn't help it.

"What the hell happened to you?" Noah yelled. "Miss fucking party girl. You're so one with God, why don't you bring Knox back?"

The crowd around them hushed for a quick moment, alarmed by Noah's outburst, his bruised eye, the slaw and shad staining his shirt. He imagined he must look like trouble. He sat down.

"You know better than to tip the scales with your sister," Dad said as Colleen took the stage, looking every bit a Tier One Class-A Irish-stepping Shad Queen. "And your friend here, all upset. What's got into you?"

Wendy, Noah saw, was crying into her napkin.

"What's wrong?" he asked. "You feel like taking a walk?"

"Leave me alone," she said.

"Come with me," he said. "You won't feel better here."

As they stood to leave, Dad said, "You'll miss Colleen if you leave now." On stage, Colleen led a troupe of girls whose bodies moved like jumping puppets from the waist down, Riverdance style. Their upper bodies were still, their smiles of plaster, their bouncing breasts and fake hair the only indicator that they were not carved from wood. Noah took Wendy away from the Revivalist tent, from the high-energy fiddling music that unaccountably made him think of sheep on speed.

Granny bit into the last of the shad, the one fish that didn't make its way onto the ground. "Sissy's the Shad Queen!" she said to no one.

"I WANT TO GO HOME," Wendy said. She'd folded her arms into her body, like a pair of wings nestled into themselves. "I can't stay here."

"Don't say that, Wendy. C'mon," Noah said.

"Your sister…"

"Poison, huh? Told you she was," Noah said.

"No. You're the poison," she said. "Why did you bring up her past like that? She's not this… Shad Queen whatever anymore."

"She'd have you believe she didn't have a past," he said.

"So what?" she said. "She's got plenty of problems without you adding to them."

"The girl I described is the one she wants to forget," he said. "She thinks turning to God's gonna save her."

"What do you care? Some people need religion to keep them on track," she said. "There's comfort in rules, in the idea of God."

"But that works only if it feels right," he said. "Let her be all one with God if it makes her happy. But you saw her. She's miserable. And she makes everyone else miserable, too."

"Oh, and you're Mr. Happy because you don't believe in God?"
Wendy said. Noah looked out at the Revivalist tent, breathing deep,
unable to answer. Wendy took Noah's hands into her own, examining
with her fingers the stiff hub of each of his fingernails, tracing the faint
vein lines. "Noah. What happened?"

Noah closed his eyes, shutting out everything: The shad fish, the
tent, the twilight sky. He wanted to say it right, so Wendy would know.

"Okay. Knox? That friend of mine? Well, he died two years ago,"
he said. "And Sissy was with him when it happened."

"Oh," Wendy's grip on his hand tightened. She curled into him.
"I'm sorry."

"We were best friends. We'd joke sometimes that we'd marry each
other's sisters, just so we could be brothers. It was silly, I guess. We were
close. He always talked about moving up to Pennsylvania with me, just
to hang out. Like he had nothing better to do down here but work at
the Gas 'N' Sip. I'd call him every couple weeks, just to say hey, and
that's all he'd talk about. The weekend he died, he was supposed to
come see me. But I had so much schoolwork I cancelled. He went out
instead with Sissy. And after, the newspaper was so vague. My mom
clipped me his obit and all it said was that he'd died. Unexpectedly.
But Colleen called me at school. Told me he'd been out with Sissy at a
college party and overdosed. That they found some mix of valium and
alcohol in his system."

It was after the wake in the pleather-hubbed booth of Duck's
Tavern that his former classmate Toby filled in Noah on what Colleen
could not, and what Sissy would not. Toby had told him how Sissy
wouldn't shut up that night, just kept going on with her brassy self
about how she'd stuffed down her pants a bag of marshmallows from
the Food Lion, thinking she was the shit, swigging from her Gallo.
And the whole time Knox was passed out on Sissy's lap. Toby said
he remembered being surprised that Knox could sleep through all
of Sissy's jay-birding and squawking, making all the boys think dirty
things about girls and marshmallows.

"Then some girl got the idea to put makeup on Knox. They put
eye shadow and lipstick on his cheeks. Everything. All over his face,"

Noah said. "And, when Sissy couldn't wake him to go home, she got some guys to get him into the backseat of her car. At some point she must have realized something was up. That he wasn't breathing, and he wasn't going to, because they ended up at the hospital. But it was too late. He'd stopped breathing somewhere between Sissy's lap and the backseat of her car. And pronounced dead, looking like a fucking clown."

Wendy brought Noah close to her. He could feel her fingertips on the ridges of his spine. "I'm so sorry," she said.

"I tried to talk to Sissy about what I'd heard, about the makeup and marshmallows. But she wouldn't get real with me. Just buffered me with blather about her recently saved soul. And then came the weight. By next Christmas, it was like Jesus himself masoned a big old wall around her."

"God. She must feel terrible," she said. "But why do you blame her?"

"A lot of people in town blame her. And, aside from the smokes, Knox never did any of that shit when I was around," Noah said. "I feel like it's my fault, too. Like if I hadn't cancelled on him that weekend, maybe he'd still be here."

Noah wiped his eyes on the shad shirts. "I'm so tired. Let's just go to the house," he said. They left the Shad Festival, holding hands as Noah drove through the darkened streets of Mewborn, back to his house. They changed into their new shad T-shirts and rested in his bed amid the bats, still holding hands, she murmuring into his ear about the plans for Peru, about the babies she wanted to have with him, how she never did get a stuffed fish of her own.

It was nearly midnight when Noah returned to Porter Bridge on his bicycle. He hadn't seen Sissy since she left the festival. He'd checked her room every hour or so, just to make sure she hadn't, yet again, stealth-climbed the stairs. What he did hear as Wendy fell asleep, was his parents coming in with Granny. They talked to her in loud voices about the same things they talked about when Noah and Sissy were kids: a glass of juice. A toothbrush. Bedtime. Eventually the television came on, and, even without leaving his bed, Noah could imagine his folks dozing in their twin easy chairs like they always had.

Now riding along the roads of his old neighborhood, Noah hardly needed the intermittent moonlight to guide him, but he was glad for it, because when the clouds passed and the moon shone it made everything ahead emerge in sharp, white-and-black contrast. Thus he saw the Porter Bridge long before it occurred to him that it was his destination. When he got there, he stopped on the curb where he and Wendy had toweled off, and walked to the center of the bridge, taking in the shine of the water below, the plunk and rush over rocks. It made grooves in the shoreline. Standing here, watching the water just after it passed under the bridge, made him feel calm, like he had never left home.

When they were kids, he and Knox had a plan to make a full run of the Neuse River, all the way to the ocean, on their inner tubes. They'd joked how they'd freak out the yachters in New Bern, move through the inlets of the Inner Banks and finally reach the Atlantic Ocean. They'd have traveled in a caravan of inner tubes: one would hold a cooler; another would hold supplies and a pair of telescopic oars; one would serve as a spare. They'd rope the whole thing together, crafting a long-distance, river-worthy black donut mass. Nothing much came of it, but the plans were still there. They'd mapped out all the coordinates on the nautical chart, they'd made the supplies list, they knew the river's shallow and deep parts; where the marinas and lighthouses were in case of bad weather.

Noah had been thinking so much about Knox that when the scent of a freshly lit cigarette hit him, he looked around, terrified, for its source. On the other side of the bridge, down along the banking, he caught sight of the cherry ember attached to the unmistakable silhouette of his sister, sitting alongside the riverbank. In the moonlight, surrounding Sissy, shone the opened wrappers of a dozen or so snack cakes. When Sissy was done with her cigarette she stood, brushing the crumbs from her body, and began to remove her clothes.

When they were kids, Noah and Knox would make liquid sand

castles, and Sissy would tag along, imitating their gripped fists of liquid sand. She was there always, with them. On the night of the Shad Queen rescue, as Sissy sobbed into Knox's arms about her lost crown, Noah remembered thinking that maybe Knox and Sissy loved each other, even then. Maybe it was love. All of it. Even when it wasn't.

Noah leaned against the steel rail of Porter Bridge as Sissy reached the river's lip and waded in. He wanted to call out to her. He wanted her life to be easier, better. But he couldn't find the words—not yet, anyway— to let Sissy know that, as she swam upstream in the rolling current of the Neuse, naked and alone, that he was watching over her, anxious in the moonlight, waiting for her return.

EVISCERATION LINE

THAT GOUT ATTACK WAS A GODSEND.

My buddies down at Golden Poultry tell me I shoulda shut things down with my ex long ago, even before things started to go south, but I never bothered. But it might have kept her in check now, like she'd know better than to send the cops my way, asking about her damn truck. Which she did, even though it's a good five years since we've been done and finished with each other.

But the swollen foot that has become my alibi has kept me off my feet and in flip-flops for a good part of this whole week. It has made me the butt of all the No Shoes, No Service jokes you can think of down at Duck's, the commentary from all the lonely buzzards who think a nightly meal consists of boiled peanuts and a six-pack of PBR, a few twists from the barmaid's orange supply. The doctor at the plant says I need to keep off my feet. Lay off the steak. And the salt. And the beer. The smokes, too. Tough orders, all of it. Last night even the TV was making me lonesome, so I stuffed my feet into my boots and tried to make it out for Duck's Shad Festival Karaoke Night competition, every song you can think of about water or fish or what have you. I love seeing all those wannabe singers get up on the mini-stage, giving "Islands in the Stream" or "Surfin' Safari" a shot, Star Search-style, unlike my brother, making it big with his guitar out in Nashville. One time these two gals got up there, did some Godawful rendition of "Bohemian Rhapsody," and all the DJ could say after their drunken train wreck of a song was, "Well. You'll won't hear that one on Cat Country Radio." And I really needed a good time tonight, would've even sat through a damn medley from ABBA, but the gravity of the swell settled into each foot, heavy like cement mob shoes. It made every step painful, if not impossible, to make. I never made it out the front door.

And now with the cops nosing around, asking if I know anything about my ex's stolen pickup, I'm glad I stayed close to home. The way they tell it, seems someone every day this week has moved her pickup to a different part of the employee lot down at the Go-Po processing plant. I laughed when they told me. Working at the same place as the ex has never been a picnic, but you hear lots of break room badmouthing and such, all sorts of things. So she'd have heard by now I was out with the gout, could barely walk anywhere, let alone drive her stick-shift truck to the far end of the lot, toss all her paperwork on the floor, and eat her plastic-wrapped lemon bars and HoHos, and hobble home, undetected.

I guess it's only natural she'd name me a suspect, if only because things didn't go so well last week after our last so-called supply closet grudge fuck, when she told me she had in her purse the papers to make our split legal. Used to be in that golden, twenty-minute stretch of coffee break, we could get back to the way we were, make good on those I Do Vows. And, after, we'd go right back to how we best function: apart. She'd revert to her hateful, manipulating ways, talking trash about me between drags in the smokeroom, me trying to reconcile what my heart knows with what my pecker feels. But this time she said she needed to move on, make it all legal, she'd pay for everything if I'd just sign. She had a pen and all. She wouldn't answer the Why Now? question except to say she needed a clean break, whatever that is. Made me wish I'd have stopped long ago keeping an eye down the evisceration line for one of her over-the-shoulder glances that said—even with her latex gloves bloody with chicken livers, dark hair back in a shower cap—to meet during break in our secret place. And there we had together our last twenty minutes of marital bliss before she left me sitting on a plastic milk crate, pants unzipped and around my ankles, clutching a good thirty pages that would legally declare us no longer together.

So of course, I broadcasted the news all over the Go-Po. Of course, the boys all felt my hangdog pain. Of course, all the women who favor my ex tried to ignore me with a knowing eye-roll, and the others began to prospect me for their spinster cousins or for themselves. Then I heard later on the line that she'd met someone else for real, one of those SUV Explorer types, some lace-curtain motherfucker who listens to Mos Def on the weekends and then goes back home to Country Club Lane.

And that's when my feet started to swell and I lost my balance and fell face down on a conveyor belt filled with chicken innards. That's when my blood pressure pills stopped working and no amount of meds could help me, and my feet blew up right there in the infirmary and the plant doctor sent me home for the rest of the week. And that's when her truck started moving from one spot in the parking lot to another, making her guess every night not only where her truck was, but who was moving it, and why. It was the perfect crime against her. Harmless, I guess, but frightening nonetheless, itching like none other could at her control freak tendency.

And I've been cursing this gout attack all week, but right now I'm grateful it's kept me from tangling with the law. I see the logic in her suspecting me—her estranged husband—who knows her better than anyone else in this town, who might still have a spare key somewhere and who knows what would get to her most. Sometimes I go by her trailer and I'm glad for everything that happened, glad I saw early on the person she was. And other times when I drive by, I feel like she must feel now, leaving the plant at five, thinking she knows just where she parked her truck, but then discovering it moved instead, unseen, by someone else who has the key to the truck and everything in it.

"Overwatering may cause carrots to fork or crack.
Keep the soil moist but not saturated."

Farmers' Almanac

FREEZER BURN

THE FOILED MEATS AND QUARTS OF FROZEN LIQUID formed a frosty wall around Lora Jones as she knelt before her open freezer. She'd gotten up early that morning to make a new batch of gazpacho and wanted to freeze another quart before she and Curtis went to the Farmers Market. But to do that, she had to shift the frozen drumsticks. The drumstick shift crowded the chicken stock containers, which in turn forced out the family-sized packs of boneless breasts and the slabs of steak. Before long the entire contents of her freezer were on the floor, which is where her husband found her.

"I had to find a place for the gazpacho," she said at the approach of Curtis's footfalls. He was already in his standard plaid shirt and jeans, ready for their Saturday. "I didn't think it would be such a project."

"Why don't we have that soup for dinner tonight?" he said.

"We already are," Lora said. She balanced a whole frozen chicken on her thigh. "This is the extra meal. For winter."

"I'm sure there's a pork chop or something waiting for a shot to defrost," he said. He leaned closer in, counting foil packs. "Just take something out."

"Don't tell me what to do," she said.

He poured himself some coffee. "I read once, in Japan, it's a sign of intelligence if you can fit multiple objects into small, contained spaces."

"Curtis? Would you please keep your jokes to yourself?"

"That's not a joke. That's a fact," Curtis said. "All I know is, if our power goes out, we'll have us one hell of a hurricane party. You just about ready to go?"

"Does it look like I'm ready to go? Give me ten minutes."

Lora finally wedged the fresh soup into the freezer, and twenty minutes later, they were on their way. Curtis sped along the roads that lined acres of cotton and tobacco fields, arriving eventually at the cement pavilion that passed in this county for a Farmer's Market. It was already packed when they pulled up to the entrance.

"I think I'll just go on to the hardware store, and come back to get you in an hour," Curtis said.

"We were going to shop together," Lora said. "The therapist said."

"Well, we got a late start to a long day," Curtis said, leaning toward Lora for a peck.

"It's only eight-thirty," she said.

"And it's getting later every minute. I'll see you in a bit," he said.

The early risers at the Mewborn Farmers Market arrived yawning in ball caps and sweatpants, holey work shirts and flip flops, milling about for local eggs and a few heads of lettuce or a sweet potato pie. Dozens of bodies moved from stall to stall in an easy, cordial way under the pavilion, out of the grasp of the morning's steamy heat. Somewhere in the din, a toddler asked for strawberries, even though it was past Labor Day. What was left of the season was mostly tough-skinned root food: Potatoes. Sweet potatoes. Carrots. Squash and more squash. A few farmers sold hand-jarred pesto and comb-in honey. Scuppernongs and string beans. Pickled okra and chow-chow. Some still had late-season tomatoes and peppers.

Lora kept her focus on the produce, knowing that any kind of eye contact with a vendor, let alone a well-timed "Morning there!" would never fail to guilt her into buying a pound or two of something she did not need, like last week's mustard greens. But she found the dozen eggs she'd been searching for and wiped out the cashbox at Compton's Farm with her twenty. Compton's teenage granddaughter, who sold her the eggs, thanked Lora with a sneering "ma'am" that made Lora vow to bring only ones and fives next time. She bought red peppers and half her tomatoes and an English cucumber for her next batch of gazpacho.

At the far side of the Farmers Market, in a corner near the back entrance, stood a man dressed in white. His thinning hair was greased back, and he held in his gloved hands a gleaming white book. It was nearing nine. Lora usually came too early to hear the man's weekly sermons, and in any case had decided he was a true optimist if he thought he'd find converts at the Mewborn Farmers Market. This week, sitting next to him, was a woman seated before a small upright wooden organ. The organ was so tiny that the woman hunched over it to play. And the woman was so comparatively sizeable that a casual glance in her direction did not at first reveal the three red wooden stool legs beneath her, so at first it appeared as though she were floating.

"This Bible," the man said, in a strong voice to no one in particular, holding up his thick book, "This! Was the only thing left the water did not touch as it passed through our Church. This! Very Bible reminded me, ladies and gentlemen, it reminded me as it lay there open on the pulpit amid the rotting wood and puddles of floodwater, of what was truly important, even as the water came and took everything else away."

The woman played encouraging notes on the organ, as though the melody agreed with the pastor, egging him on. Curtis and Lora had moved to Mewborn a year after Hurricane Nestor destroyed the homes lining the Neuse River. Nearly everyone they'd met had a story about their survival and loss in the flood that followed. Curtis worked at the hospital as an anesthesiologist's assistant. When his part-time work went permanent, Lora had found work as a collection agent for

U-Pay Co., and in spite of her hating to cold-call errant bill payers—
she could never filter out the apologetic tone in her voice—she had
quit looking at the Sunday classifieds. She'd heard the bulk of the
flood tales over the phone. Nestor was the main excuse—or reason—
for quite a few folks whose names and numbers cropped up on her
database. And still, the parameters of her job required her to demand
from them money they simply did not have.

The organ had a breathing, nasal drone that harkened bagpipes
rather than the bright notes of a piano or the tinny tone of a keyboard.
It had a breathing chamber, like a bullfrog's bellow. Lora moved closer.
The man's words grew more forceful as the organ wheezed out notes.

"The waters divided, smashed, destroyed, even. Destroyed! But
it brought us together, too. Those waters brought our neighbors...
together. It brought our churches...together. White and black, we
were all...together, ladies and gentlemen! We lifted ourselves up! We
lifted UP, I say, and when everything was in disaster, when all of your
food was rotten and your mattress was growing mold in a tree in your
backyard and all your magazines and toothbrushes and kitty litter and
sandwich meat came charging out of your house, pushed by the Water
of God—the Water that beat down your door and charged through
and cast everything precious to you out into the street, for the world
to see—your embarrassment of riches! Your embarrassment, ladies
and gentlemen! All the things you had and owned—those things you
thought you owned—those photographs and books and armoires and
televisions sets?" Sweat clotted through his white suitcoat. "Where are
they now? Where are they? They are nothing but memories!"

Lora envisioned all of her and Curtis's things in their front yard.
All those yogurt containers dripping chicken stock on the lawn, their
furniture and vintage Stones albums, their eight years of joint tax
returns like postage stamps cast across the grass. Just then, Becky
McAllister clicked past the preacher in high-heels and her hot pink
can-do Capri pants. Her green straw beach bag concealed her fresh
produce. Becky's husband James worked at the same hospital as Curtis,
and she'd heard Becky had battled with cancer a few years back, but

she'd apparently rebounded. Lora noticed the glossy white tips of Becky's nails and rearranged her ball cap.

"Hey, Lora," Becky said. "Getting your dose of religion?"

"That Bible he's holding is the only thing in his church the flood didn't get," Lora said.

Becky snorted. "Apparently every Bible in Mewborn has some miracle flood savior story. Some reporter was stupid enough to put it in the paper. Now it's one of those suburban legends."

The man in white clutched the Bible, which did look brand-new. Even his tennis shoes had a glossy spaceman shine to them, like rock-hard Adidas.

"Hey, you'll never guess," Becky said. "James and I were at the Collins' last night? For drinks? And Shar and Cran were there and guess who didn't drink the wine?"

Lora felt her stomach turn at Becky's singsong voice. The Collins had a party?

"Um, who?" Lora asked.

"Shar! She sipped water out of a wine stem all night. Didn't even bother to share the news. I think that's rude. I mean, if you're pregnant, you're pregnant. The whole world isn't going to stop for a baby," Becky said. "Just out with the news and move on, that's what I say."

"Maybe they aren't sure yet," Lora said, still thinking about what the man had said about lost toothbrushes and photographs. How the world might just stop for a baby. Just then, two children in matching striped shirts and fairy wings ran toward the organist. The woman's hair was thin and slick, like the man's, and the flesh of her arms jiggled in sync with the movement of her hands. Both of her arms had a half-dozen marks, age-old scars about three inches long, just under the crook of her elbow. Becky squinted at the organ.

"That thing looks familiar. I think Harold Crossen, my old yoga teacher? back in the Army? played one of those in our yoga class. Some lady—not this one, for sure—did some chanting. Kundalini style? She was all yippie-yi-yay, rolling her tongue, and all that," Becky said.

"Where would you find a Kundalini organ around here?" Lora asked.

"Maybe a dime-store find? Who knows? I think it's from India, or something. Strange to see one here at the farmers market," Becky said. "You'd think a Hindu music machine wouldn't do so well with the Baptists."

The man turned his attention toward Lora and Becky. He spoke over them, over their heads, as though two very tall people loomed behind them. Lora sensed he was speaking to them directly and then realized they were among just a handful of people who had stopped shopping to listen.

"Let us give thanks that each of you can be here now, choosing your tomatoes for your lunch! For your B!L!T! Sandwiches! Choosing your dessert pies for your children!" he said. "Yes, ladies and gentlemen, we lost much in our lives, but did we lose our will to go on? To keep having? To keep wanting? No, ladies and gentlemen, we did not. And even though, sadly, my church is no longer fit for visitors, I certainly am. My body is my temple, and I choose to welcome you in! And each of you today can choose the same! We! Are making a choice!"

He closed his eyes and extended his arms as he prayed over the market as the organ droned on. Becky sighed and swept her sunglasses from her face to atop her head. "And my choice? is to continue shopping," she said. "See ya, Lora."

Becky disappeared into the crowd. Lora still had some change from her split twenty and looked around the market for one last buy. She spied pumpkins at Craydle's stand, the first of the season, and suddenly all Lora could think of was November. Curtis had suggested they ask a few of the other North Carolina transplants to Thanksgiving that year. She thought of the people seated around her table eating pumpkin pie: Becky and her husband and their kids. The Collinses. Shar and Cran and the precious bump in Shar's abdomen. Maybe Syona from U-Pay. The man in white began to thunder again about choice. She gave Jo Craydle her last six dollars and selected a huge pumpkin for pie filling. With a half-dozen plastic bags dangling from her wrists, Lora balanced the pumpkin between her hip and stomach and went back to the woman playing the organ.

The two children were still there, kneeling near the woman as she played. Their eyes were fixed on her left hand, which pushed and released, pushed and released, a black flap on the back of the organ.

"Is that a piano?" one of the children asked, a Bugs Bunny-caliber carrot cramming his mouth.

"No, love, it's a harmonium," the woman said, her voice hushed.

"That's not a harmonica," the other child said.

"That's right, it ain't," the woman said. "Harm-o-nium."

"Why does it breathe like that?"

"When I push this flap, the air gets sucked inside the box. The reeds inside fill up. When I hit the organ keys, it lets out the air and makes music," the woman said. Harmonium. Lora had never heard that word before. It made her think of trillium, ammonium, sodium. An element for harmony. Harmonium. A noble gas. The essence of a musical note. She thought about molecules, splitting and filling the air, of whirring spectrometers and funnels that could manipulate and freeze substances, of a rock-solid Walt Disney suspended in a room somewhere in Orlando or Anaheim, lying in wait for a serum that would give him life so he could draw more cartoons of rats and dogs who wear pants and drive cars.

"But what does…" the child asked.

The woman held up her hand. "Now, hush. I have come all the way from Georgia to play for my dear brother Silas' sermons. You just listen in and enjoy yourselves." Lora could almost see all the oxygen at the farmers market suddenly sucked in the harmonium, all of it trapped and shaped and forced to be filled with notes, to be moved and to resonate, even for just a second or two: a thousand molecules assuming the form, holding the note, and dissipating in an instant. It was like those flash gatherings she'd read about, where people would convene and eat a banana at a Starbucks in Sevilla or wave a pink feather at exactly 3:58 p.m. at an Origins makeup counter at Neiman-Marcus in San Francisco.

The woman looked up from her organ and caught Lora's eye.

"Are these yours, honey? 'Cause they are smart! Just loaded with questions," she said.

"I don't have any children," Lora said. "We… can't."

The woman's smile softened. "Lord have mercy on you."

Lora wasn't sure if she should thank the woman, so she just gave her an uncertain smile and turned away, feeling the brunt of the pumpkin's weight, startled by what she'd just admitted. Lora had never said aloud they couldn't have babies, not even to Curtis. And they'd tried for a while, but even after a few months, sex had devolved from a somewhat pleasant recreational activity to an obligation. It wasn't long after that they'd stopped altogether and would not admit to each other what Lora had told the organist. She shifted the pumpkin from one hip to the other. The clock on the pavilion wall told her Curtis would be here soon.

"Have a bless day!" the woman called over her notes.

Lora left the harmonium drone and waited outside to watch the boys in the adjacent field play rugby. They ran in herds, and every few so often would convene in scrum, arms and backs intertwined in a huge huddle, like a massive jellyfish waiting for an egg to drop amid the clamor of moving, kicking legs. In an instant, with their parents' meager applause as a soundtrack, they would disperse across the field to track the ball in play. Lora could never stand rugby, never saw the point, even as a child, of playing any game that could result in being bashed in the face with a ball. Her brother had played through college, and much of her girlhood had been spent in a dewy field somewhere in Vermont watching boys play. She remembered kicking at melting gray-white piles of months-old snow, of wet mittens in March after attempting a sidelines cartwheel. Lora and Curtis had hardly seen snow since they had moved south, save for an occasional flurry on a cold day. September here felt more like June.

Lora spotted their Volvo entering the driveway. She walked from the lip of the field toward the parking lot and motioned with her chin for Curtis to release the hatch of the trunk. He didn't catch the signal and instead pulled up alongside her and popped open the passenger door.

"I need to put this pumpkin in the trunk," she said.

"Lora? I'm sorry. I need to get back to the house. There's stuff in the trunk. Just get in."

Lora sighed her pissed-off sigh, as she lowered herself into the car, the pumpkins weight square on her bladder.

Curtis turned to her. "What?"

"As though two seconds of opening the trunk will affect everything," she said.

"It will. The trunk is full of mulch and grass seed. I need to get home. Gotta get the lawn cut. Why did you buy that thing anyway?"

"What thing?"

"The pumpkin on your lap?"

"I thought I would boil it down for pies this afternoon. For Thanksgiving. For our party."

Curtis adjusted the rearview mirror and pulled out of the parking lot. "Lora. Thanksgiving is two months away. Why are you buying pumpkins now? We don't even know if anyone will come."

Lora adjusted the pumpkin in her lap. The plastic bags rustled at her feet.

"Even if they don't, we'll eat it this winter. When there's no fresh food. When we're too tired to leave the house. Or, if there's a blizzard, or something."

"Firstoff?" Curtis said. "There are no blizzards down here, and even if there were, the last thing we would crave is frozen mashed pumpkin. Second: grocery stores are filled with food every day of the week. And third. That pumpkin isn't a pumpkin pie pumpkin. Only the little ones are. So you can de-seed and boil and mash this thing all you want. It will be the worst tasting pie you ever eat."

They drove home, silent. Lora hadn't moved. The pumpkin weighed down her abdomen, pushing into her pelvis. She could hardly breathe as they pulled into their driveway. Curtis came around to her side of the car and opened the door.

"C'mon, Lora. Let's unpack this stuff. I got a long day," he said. "Hedges. The lawn."

Lora didn't move. She had to pee. She contemplated forty-pound bags of kitty litter and dozens of Moon Pies and unripe watermelon and the man in white who had lost his church in a flood. She could imagine Shar at the Collins' party, refusing wine in her coy way, pushing back her amber curls to reveal that flushed, expectant complexion. She looked out, over the dashboard and beyond the windshield and could see the grass needed mowing and mulching and soon the pinecones would have to be gathered and it all began to descend upon her, like the constant, anxious gnawing of a rat. She thought of the woman, the preacher's sister from Georgia, who played the harmonium in the pavilion, of her congruous notes aligned like the shiny golden teeth on a corncob, of every molecule in the pavilion stretched with music. Lora longed to see her again, to ask her about her scars, to help her breathe life into the harmonium and push the bellows open and shut, open and shut. This was what she murmured, what Curtis did not hear:

"I want my molecules to sing."

"Lora? What? Let's go. Look, we can toast the pumpkin seeds. Have an early Jack-o-Lantern, or something, okay?"

Lora scooped up the handles of her shopping bags and clutched the pumpkin in her arms as she maneuvered out of the car. The morning haze was gone and Lora could feel the hot sharp angles of the day, the sun boring down into the Volvo. Curtis moved to take the pumpkin from Lora's arms as she emerged from the car. Her grip grew tight around it.

"C'mon, Lora. Let me take it. I'll bring it in."

"No," Lora said.

Curtis grabbed the stem as Lora edged toward the woodpile that bordered the house. She fell back and everything—the carton of eggs, the tomatoes, the pepper, the pumpkin, the cord of wood: all of it lay scattered in plastic across the pavement.

"Lora?" Curtis said, moving toward the spilt bags. "I'm sorry."

The pumpkin's firm roundness was distorted and broken open from the fall. Its seeds lay scattered, the pulp on the driveway. It would soon stiffen and bake dry in the sun. The eggs oozed yellow from the plastic bag onto the grass. Lora ran into the house, leaving Curtis to collect the groceries, to restack the fallen bundle of wood.

Let me breathe, Lora thought as she entered the kitchen. Just let me breathe. She opened the door of the freezer. She could feel the sweat on her face stiffen as whorls of the bright cold light cast around her, the lingering notes of the harmonium still coursing through her body. The cool air filled with the stale scent of dried blood and stiff meat and months of frozen vegetables, but even so, Lora breathed deep, taking stock of all that she had collected and lost.

GREEN MONSTER

THE GARDEN WAS A SMALL GARDEN. It was the garden that came with the house. A vegetable garden that, with wood and weed and pest, required frequent tending, even on game days, and Wylie Burns could not stand to be in it without a hip flask tucked neat in the seat pocket of his pants. The folds of his hands were creased with dirt, dirt too slick, thanks to the rain, even to be called dirt. Mud, Wylie thought, as he watched it harden to a pale paste on his palm, *I am covered in mud.*

The rain had blown in from the northwest sky hours earlier. The drops from the rain had loosed the loam, and the blind roots that never stopped their search for more footage, for expansion, probed for growth and thrived on the moist soil. The rain, arriving earlier, unsuspected, in the dark, fell in drops onto the leeks and the lace of bean leaves and into the folds of past-season lettuce. The rain beaded on the wax of pepper and pooled in the intersection of the stem and fruit of the tomatoes. The moisture from the pools would seep into the fruit later that day. It would force a split in its last stage of ripening.

Wylie heard the back door slam and knew Florine was walking toward him. She would be holding a tall glass of yellow liquid. The rubber bottoms of her thin canvas sneakers squealed on the damp grass as she walked. The mud spread to Wylie's forehead as he wiped the sweat from his brow. He thought of the Sox game, of someone else sitting on his barstool, arm crooked around the waist of the waitress, asking for more. He thought of the small mound of ash and stubs that would grow in the glass dish with each inning, and at the stretch the barmaid would clear the ash from the dish. Wylie's dad once brought him and his brothers to Fenway, a scalped ticket game for nosebleed bleacher seats. The Sox lost that day, just as Wylie lost everything, years later, on a whirlwind whim to drop his life in Somerville and start one in Mewborn with Florine. The Sox remained the sole tether to his old life. And for what? For a never-ending cycle of garden and woman and mud that for once made him understand his old man.

Wylie bent over a network of weeds that had crept from the crabgrass and infiltrated the garlic barriers. The weeds had strangled the carrots. They had undercut the eggplant and honeydew vines and had given inroads to underground crawlers from the lawn. Wylie pulled at a weed near his foot and saw a half-dozen shiny pupae just under its uprooted vine. He squinted up into the bright day. Florine came to the edge of the garden.

"Wy… Brought you a drink."

"You brought me drink?"

"You don't want a drink?"

"I have a drink. I just happen not to be drinking it."

"That old flask."

"Enough about the flask."

"What? I hardly mentioned it."

"It's enough that you did." Wylie pulled at another weed.

"You mentioned it first. You said you already had a drink."

"But you said flask. 'That old flask.'"

"You meant flask when you said you had a drink. What does it matter?"

"Give me the glass."

FLORINE HANDED WYLIE THE GLASS. He drank because he was thirsty. He drank because it was hot out, because the weeds were always there, because they always needed routing. He drank because the larvae would remain burrowed underground, curled into donuts, lining the soil. He would see to that. He drank because he hated her, hated moving down here for her, hated her reminding him of what she gave up just to be with him, bygod that bitch always knew how to sink her damn claws right in. He could take whatever she gave him. She kept him penned in, here, scratching at weeds, covered in dirt. He kicked dirt over the pupae and finished the beer in one gulp. He handed the glass to her and returned to the weeds and the waxy peppers and split tomatoes and the melon vine and aging lettuce. She always found a way to keep him from forgetting.

THE COLD FRONT

WHEN WE SAW LORA JONES, she was standing on the lip of her un-shoveled driveway off Frog Level crossing, howling as she removed what was left of her long underwear. It was the day after a surprise blizzard, a Saturday, and she wore nothing but her boots. She screeched at her husband Curtis about Swiss Miss snow bunnies and slutty Barbie dolls. She hurled many snowballs. She cursed, loudly. When we turned down the radio, we caught "that nasty e-mail-sending whore" and "why won't you just listen?" Curtis was silent. He shoveled snow.

We were out for a ride with the kids after the storm, giving Becky's minivan a first-run test in the snow, when we came across the Jones. I slowed down and flipped up the shade attachment for my glasses to get the full effect.

"Lookit there, honey. A snow queen," I said. I had to grin at the sight of her. Lora Jones looked pretty darn good. The cool air had hardened her nipples to a deep pink and her muscular, golden body

must have been covered in goose bumps. Her hair was flyaway blonde.
Along with scattered stacks of magazines, which blew about in the
wind, her clothes littered the frozen lawn. I rolled down the window.

"James, don't," Becky said. "The kids!"

"Hey, is everything all right there? You need any help?" I asked.

Lora Jones turned toward us and screamed, "Haven't you ever seen
a naked woman before? Get the hell out of here!"

"I don't think the Joneses need our help, dear," I said, trying to keep
a straight face.

"This isn't funny, James. I'm calling the police. We can't have this in
our neighborhood," Becky said. She glanced back at Susie and Paul,
asleep in their car seats.

"Give her a break, Beck. There's a time when you'd have stripped
down to your skivvies yourself just to make a point." As it was, Becky
had been wearing the same grey sweatpants and duck boots for three
days. Her navy blue vest puffed up and distorted her top half. You'd
never guess that under her L.L. Bean look, a tattoo of blue stars lined
the upper ridge of her hipbones, or that she used to strut around
Duck's Tavern on Thursday nights when she was home from Fort
Bragg, singing karaoke in tight jeans and a tube top.

"That time is over," Becky said. She pawed through her bag for her
cell phone.

Lora Jones had begun to stomp on magazines—I could see Playboy
and Hustler among them—as Curtis continued to shovel around his
Volvo, his wide face expressionless. For a while, he used to help doctors
anesthetize patients down at Mewborn Hospital. I would see him
walking through the lobby from time to time when Lora was getting
her chemo treatments, or in the hospital parking lot, and we'd talk
some, as neighbors do, about dogs and lawns and such. Then I heard
down at Duck's that he'd got into the online porn business after he
got fired from the hospital. No one knew why he'd been fired, but I
just couldn't imagine his thick fingers sticking needles into people on
an operating table any more than I could see him selling porn in his
basement. He seemed too numb. Thick fingers, or something. Even
now, he did not react to his wife's snowballs, or her accusations, not

even when she pushed him down in the snow, straddled his stomach, and shook him by the collar of his coat, screaming, "I just want you to see me!"

Becky focused on her phone, thumbs pushing buttons. "No service," she said. "Damn."

"Put that phone away. Can't you see they're having it out?" I said, pulling out of neutral. "Let's get out of here."

As soon as we got home, Becky stepped out of the minivan with the phone still pressed to her ear and headed indoors. The kids woke up, so I took them out of their car seats and let them loose in the front yard. Susie followed her mother, while Paul went to check on the snowman we'd built this morning. It was almost time for dinner, but I didn't feel like going in the house. Instead I found my flask under the front seat of my truck, took a swig before I tucked it into my coat pocket, and joined Paul before the snowman.

Our snowman is an ordinary snowman. He's got a blue scarf wound around his neck and an old Burger King crown on his head. He's sloppy-dumpy, like any other front-yard suburban snowman, with charcoal features and an unpeeled carrot for a nose. I won't waste briquettes on buttons, or break branches for arms. It doesn't matter, really. In the end, arms or no arms, top hat or paper crown, all snowmen will eventually look alike: frozen and sagging into the grass, one big puddling mess.

I'd promised Paul earlier we could build another snowman—this time, a girl—before the snow melted.

"Then we'll have the set," I'd said. "A snowman. And a snow ma'am." I was in high school the last time a snowstorm like this blew through Mewborn, so I figured Paul and Susie and I could make the best of it, with snowmen and sledding. We'd even made a last-minute bread-and-milk run to the Piggly Wiggly on Highway Eleven, just to see the idling plow trucks. Right now, the last thing I wanted to do was go inside and deal with Becky and her cop-calling antics.

"What do you think?" I said. "Time we get that snow ma'am underway?"

Paul nodded. Together we started to push snow into a mound. I could feel the chill of the air through my clothes. I took off my gloves and scooped snow into my hands. I felt my palms go numb and thought about how cold Mrs. Jones must have been. What was she feeling out there? God, she looked amazing. Why did she strip like that? I contemplated this until I spied Paul's blue mittens on the ground next to me. I shook the slush out of my hands, then his.

"Come here, silly," I said as I wiped his hands on the cuff of my pants. I helped him put on his mittens. The front door slammed. Becky and Susie were walking toward us. Becky's brows formed a prim double arch over her wide, blue eyes. Her hair was still cropped short, even though she stopped chemo almost three years ago.

"What is your problem?" she said.

"Paul took off his mittens," I said. "I'm just getting them back on."

"That's not what I meant," she said. "You know dinner will be ready soon."

"It will be too dark for snowmen after dinner," I said. I tugged at each of Paul's mitten cuffs, for emphasis. "This won't take long."

I helped Paul scoop more snow. He patted it down with a plastic beach shovel. Becky stood there, waiting.

"Don't you want to know what the cops said?" she asked.

"Not particularly," I said.

"Well, they're busy with calls from the snowstorm, but Sheriff Stanton said they'd send someone by," she said.

"So someone can't be naked around here without you calling the chief of police, is that it?"

Paul started to form what looked like a huge snowball for the midsection. I found my flask and took another sip.

"Curtis Jones is a pervert," Becky said. "She's no better. Indecent exposure in a snowstorm? Seriously. What's she trying to prove?"

"You hardly know them," I said. I helped Paul lift the midsection onto the base. "I don't see why we got to get in on the tit patrol in the middle of nowhere. Getting mucked in their mess sure as hell won't solve ours."

"What does that mean, exactly?" Becky asked.

I stopped helping Paul and leaned on my shovel. "What I'm saying is, their problems are not ours. And we got plenty of our own," I said. "There's no need to interfere."

"Well, you make a lot of sense," Becky said. She was trying to keep her voice low, but I could feel the heat in her words. She grabbed my arm and dragged me away from the kids. "Some naked bimbo starts screaming at her porno pimp husband in the middle of a snowstorm, and you blame me for their problems and ours?"

"God, Becky. Don't put words in my mouth," I said. "I don't blame you for…"

"Nothing would be solved, you know, if I got buck naked in front of the world," she said.

When I spoke, I too lowered my voice and moved in closer to her. "I wish you could hear yourself talk, Becky. Because seeing any part of you naked might do the trick," I said. "I haven't touched you, let alone fuck you for what, two years?" She looked away, toward the kids, her arms folded across her chest.

"I'm just speaking the truth," I said. "I feel like I'm still paying for a two-year-old mistake."

"You are," she said, grabbing hold of a branch as she walked away. When she let go, the snow from the branch came down over me in powdery chunks. Susie ran toward the backyard. As Becky tracked after our girl, I walked over to Paul and watched him finish the snow ma'am's head.

Two years of no sex was a generous estimate. After Becky's operation, we tried once. It was a few months after her mother left and she was done with the chest packs and the painkillers and the drain tubes. After she decided she'd rather put the kids through college than pay for breast reconstruction. She said she felt ready. She said she wanted me. I knew she'd be changed; I knew she'd have no breasts. But nothing prepared me for when our bodies actually touched. In the dark and through her nightgown, I pulled my hand away from her body. It was a reflex, involuntary, but she left our bed and nothing would convince her to come back. And I haven't touched her since. After that, she surrounded herself with the kids and made it so we never got a moment alone. She usually sleeps in Susie's room, or on the couch; I go out to Duck's most nights to forget about it, or to conferences for my job at the hospital, and come home so late that it doesn't matter where we sleep. Apologies make it worse: Sorry for touching her. Sorry for pulling away. Sorry for the cancer. Sorry, now, for mentioning it.

Paul turned toward me and giggled.

"Daddy, you look like a snowman," he said.

"Thank you," I said, brushing off the snow. "Say, you got a carrot on you? I can't smell a darn thing."

I went into the garage for the bag of charcoal. I handed the bag to Paul and broke the first snowman's carrot in two. As I watched Paul wedge each coal into the snowman's face and place the half-carrot for its nose, I couldn't help but imagine that Mrs. Jones would probably want a guy like me. Someone who'd pay attention to her, like she wanted. Maybe she'd lean in with a cheesecake pose on the hood of my minivan. Or she'd sit on a bearskin rug in the snow, her hair in two braids brushing each breast, her knees bent, each heel touching the lower corners of the rug, letting me see the pink folds beyond her dark down. Her boots would still be on, and she'd beg me to take her, right there, in front of the snowman. Or in front of her husband, who would continue to shovel out his Volvo, no matter what. And everything I'd ever felt would pour into her. And she would take in all of me, accept me completely, with her eyes open, wanting more.

"Daddy? How do we tell it's a girl?"

"How do we tell what's a girl?" I said, face reddening.

"You said she's a snow ma'am?" he said.

"So I did. Hold on," I said. I returned to the garage to find a few ribbons in the Christmas box that I had yet to bring to the attic. I pushed past last month's ceramic fir trees and gilded stars and ratty red stockings and focused on finding ribbons. Then I went back out.

"Here," I said, handing him the ribbons. "Put them on her head. Then we'll know."

Paul grinned as he took them. Leaning on my shovel, I watched him wrap the ribbons, green and gold, around her head.

"She's beautiful," I said. When he was done, Paul grabbed my hand and led me toward Becky and Susie.

"Mommy, we made a lady out of snow!" Paul said.

Becky gave me a sharp look. In a phony, loving-mother voice, she said, "A girl snowman. That's great, sweetie. Now whose idea was that?"

"Daddy's. He said it's a snow ma'am," Paul said.

"We've got the happy pair right there on the lawn," I said. "Mister and missus." I sounded, for Paul's sake, friendly and upbeat. Like a guy who eats cereal for breakfast every morning. Who brings flowers home to brighten up the kitchen.

"Well, I thought it was just a plain old snow…person," Becky said.

"No, it's a girl," Paul said.

"Let's go see," she said, still looking at me, her eyes sending out all the reformed whore, fake church-lady meanness they could muster. As we approached the snow lady, I said, "Now, Beck, don't you go calling the cops. I can assure you the snow ma'am is fully clothed."

It would have been one thing if Becky had just slapped me or if she had just called me an asshole in front of the kids, then went into the house. I would have preferred that. But instead, she formed two snowballs from the snow ma'am's midsection, held them to her chest, and said, "I'm sure you know exactly where to put these, James." Then she threw them both at me, dead-on.

The children giggled.

"Mommy hit Daddy with a snowball," said Paul in a singsong voice, then Susie threw a handful of snow at Paul and soon they were romping and laughing. Snow was flying everywhere as Becky and I stood there, arms crossed, glaring at each other.

I turned away from her, eventually, and as I did, the snowman's expression caught my eye. It looked to me like the charcoal had been arranged so the snowman held a smirking, leering grin. As though the snowman found Becky's snowball stunt really funny.

I reached for the shovel and sideswiped the snowman's head with it. His head hit the snow ma'am straight on, and her head toppled. Becky backed away, and I ignored Paul's wails for me to stop. I couldn't stop pummeling the snow-torsos with my fists. I stomped on their heads. Bows and charcoal smiles and the paper crown and carrots and scarf all scattered across the lawn.

"Why do you have to ruin everything?" Becky said.

It was only after I realized I was alone on the lawn that I realized Becky brought the kids inside the house, away from me. I pounded on the door, my housekey useless on account of the deadbolt.

"Why can't you see I'm sorry?" I yelled. I jiggled the doorknob one last time before I walked toward the minivan. "I'm sorry!"

On my way I saw a lump of coal uncrushed from the snowman's grin. I kicked it. I kicked it again. What I really needed was to go for a drive.

I DROVE FOR A FEW HOURS ALONG THE BACK ROADS outside of Mewborn as nightfall arrived. We never see this much snow in Eastern Carolina, and usually it shuts down nearly everything, especially where we live, some five miles out in the county. The TV warned it might take a few days for the plows to come through our neighborhood, but the truck came by the house this morning, first thing. Eventually I got the courage to drive by the Jones' house. It was dark, save for a dim red light from a window on the second floor. Curtis's Volvo was gone from the driveway.

I drove by a few more times before I stopped the minivan on the side of the road and rolled down the window to feel the night air on my face. I idled there a long time, staring at the bare, frozen lawn, and the shoveled driveway. I tried to imagine Lora Jones somewhere in that house, alone, too brave for her own good. Or Becky, deciding it was her duty to police the neighborhood. I guess if someone drove by and saw me beating on a snowman with a shovel, she'd call the sheriff, too. I tried to recreate the hot and heavy snow queen fantasy of this afternoon, but instead my mind kept drifting back to Becky, who was probably asleep on the couch or on the recliner in Susie's room. The last image that came to my mind as I drifted off was of me asleep in

Becky's arms. When I awoke a couple hours later, the minivan was still idling, and I had just enough gas to get back to the house. The light in the Joneses' house had been turned off. The Volvo was now in the driveway. I shifted the minivan into reverse and drove home.

When I pulled into our driveway, I saw the wind had carried one of Paul's ribbons across the yard. I chased it nearly back to the road and wrapped it around my neck. The remains of our snow people lay in a pile on the front yard. I didn't bother to check the door to see if Becky had finally unlocked it. Instead, I knelt in the yard, collecting snow, gathering it into a mound. Soon I'd shaped it into a snowman. Then I made another, and another. Soon there was a village on the front lawn: icy three-plop replicas, dozens of them, a small army cold and sturdy in the moonlight.

By the time I finished, my knuckles were scraped and frozen, fingers numb. I was sweaty. Becky came outside then, in her blue vest, the cuffs of her pajama pants tucked into her duck boots. She picked up a gold ribbon, shook it off, and wrapped it criss-cross around the head of the snow person nearest the house.

"Why don't you come inside?" she said.

"I'm not done here," I said. That was true. I still had to pat down the base I was working on, make it concave, like a platter ready to receive the midsection.

"Let me help you," she said. She picked up the charcoal bag and began to place eyes on ice. She made black, three-point smiles on the frozen men.

"I'm fine here," I said.

"James," she said. "You're not fine."

I stood up. "Look. I don't give a shit about the cancer. And you always have to be so, so fucking proud or something. So perfect. All the time. And I'm just..."

Becky looked out at the lawn, as though she was searching for something. I stopped making the torso to look, too, to see what she saw. The lawn was dark and muddy in the spaces between the snowmen. It looked like there was no ground beneath them, and each one was fixed and frozen in its own world, floating in space in the darkness.

She approached one snowman and broke off a section of its head, forming it into a ball. Cupping her hands with care around the ice, she threw the ball into the night.

"It's enough," she said. She made and threw another snowball. "You're enough, all right?"

She bent down and formed more snowballs.

"Cut it out, Becky," I said, annoyed that she'd hacked the snowman's head like that.

This time, she aimed for me. I ducked.

"You're getting snow everywhere," I said, even though I knew I sounded like an old lady. Snow got down my neck and stuck in my stubble. "I'm warning you," I added.

"What'll happen?" said Becky.

She was holding a pair of snowballs at chest level. Crouching behind one of the snowmen, I made a snowball from its middle.

"All, I'm saying is, you'd better watch it," I said. I hurled a snowball at her. It missed. I tossed three more, but only one nicked her vest.

I found the flask I'd tucked into my coat and took a swig.

"Any left in that for me?" Becky said as she threw a snowball. It hit my chest dead-on. She advanced toward me like a stealthy soldier, shielding herself.

"Not if you're my enemy," I said. I threw another round her way, maneuvering through the yard, trying to avoid Becky's barrage, until we'd dismantled all the snowmen and only one remained for each of us. I peeked over the frozen midsection of mine, clutching my flask; Becky emerged from behind her snowman to face me. I stood and extended the flask in her direction; she took a sip, then tucked the flask into the pocket of her vest. I stepped closer to her. She sighed and stared at the sky. Taking a breath, I reached toward her and rested my palm on her chest, over her heart. She placed her hand over mine, and we stood together amidst our toppled bodies.

VERBINDUNG DURCH ANGST

A FUNERAL PHOTOGRAPH OF THE FAMOUS GERMAN THINKER HAD arrived that morning in the mail. It arrived protected, wrapped in a cellophane sleeve and sealed in a white, aerogramme envelope with a black border, marked with a series of colorful cancelled stamps. Air Mail. International Air Mail. All the way from Køln. Caldon, who had moved to his mother's family home in the Vermont woods, to escape the city, and his wife Mary, sorted through the mail that morning as he had every morning for the past two years: on the can, with a cup of chicory coffee perched on the sill of the window.

With the letters on his lap, he kept his penis between his legs, out of the way, angled toward the bowl, a courtesy to both the correspondence and his unpredictable bladder. When he looked down—which, on occasion, he did, once it occurred to him—he could not dismiss a distinct sensation that his grizzle might conceal some undiscovered feminine crevice. But he'd always push away the thought as quickly as it came.

The German, Helmut Krämer, was a former classmate and neighbor from nearly fifty years ago, and had eventually made a name for himself at Columbia. Or so he'd heard. As teenagers on the lower East Side, Helmut, who came from hearty German stock, had always looked older than Caldon, broader in both shoulder and jawline, even though Caldon was the elder by a few months and the taller by a few inches. Helmut had aged, of course, but somehow, even while dead, he now appeared in the photo looking younger, more virile than Caldon. And here I am, Caldon thought, flipping over the photo, squinting at the light scrawl of German on the back, still competing with a dead man. He wasn't that old, Caldon thought. Same age as me. The photo was black and white, taken with natural lighting, he guessed, on account of the slight blur and haze and peculiar exaggerated glow about the face, like a spot exposure. Caldon could make out a large, complex ear attached to a long, pillowed lobe, as though Helmut somehow, through the photo, could hear Caldon and his grumblings amid his bathroom business. The ear seemed disproportionate to Helmut's pinched lips and grim, broken-nose profile. Caldon supposed the distortion was on account of the positioning of his head, adorned with trademark but now useless glasses. That bastard always did have big ears, he thought. A big dick, too, recalling the countless gang showers they'd been forced to take after gym class at Taft, the whipped towels and idiot horseplay of a bunch of young men who'd never yet even heard the word "homosexual," much less know what it meant. They didn't have vocabulary for gays back then that he knew of, but that all changed. How quick had it changed. His own son became a daughter, so who was he to say otherwise? From Joseph to Josie over winter break. Transgender at Christmas. Just like that. He pressed the photo to his face and inhaled the darkroom chemicals, the margin of the thick paper carefully cut to accommodate the handwritten note below. The writing was in German, written in the sloping hand of his ancient mother somewhere in Køln, who, at nearly ninety, likely drank daily the brine of pickled cucumbers and would live the rest of her years, he supposed, buying vegetables and mutton at an open-air market, toting a steel hamper-style shopping cart.

So this is what the dead look like, Caldon thought, taking in the endless leaves outside his window, now almost blushed with the season but attached still to branches alongside the scrum of tiny birds that sat in caucus, deliberating their southward migration. The Keith Jarrett album from the other room bloomed in a well of applause and paused when Caldon stood, the photograph pressed between his finger and thumb, as the bills and circulars and even the onionskin aerogramme envelope scattered across the tile floor. He pulled up his overalls and abandoned his coffee on the ledge, thinking only about the dead German in the open coffin, and the fragile, foreign penmanship that conveyed the news that he could not read. He had to talk to Willow.

The house he'd inherited, to the consternation of his elder and now-dead siblings, save for Willow, who got the Manhattan apartment from their mother's will, was little more than a cabin, not designed or properly insulated for cold weather use, but he'd managed. As kids they'd slept outdoors every night in pup tents, popping into the sweltering kitchen to see their mother, who rarely left it, perpetually cooking for a family of six. But its potbelly stove and snug size gave him and Mary seasons of escape with Joseph, before he became Josie. It wasn't far from a lake, and the one thin power line from the lone outpost post kept the radio going, the coffee heated, and, depending on the season, a fan or space heater whirring full-blast. His father, who grew up in Eastern Carolina but came to New York as a young man, enjoyed keeping a garden, but Caldon wasn't one much for yard work or lawn care, so the natural bramble of once-maintained blackberry bushes interspersed with a few heirloom tomato plants and carrots and overtook the bulk of what would have been a yard, making the June harvest sweet indeed. So sweet that his fingers for a full month were permanently purple, his hands and ankles still healing from scratches from thorns. The cabin brought him, at sixty-six, back into his kid element, and so he flipped the Jarrett album, and let the second half of the concert take him as he stuffed some coins and a twenty for the paper into his overalls pocket to walk down the deserted tree-lined road, barefoot and still holding Helmut's photograph, to the pay phone at the gas station. He'd read somewhere that the piano Jarrett had wanted for the concert—in Køln, Caldon realized, what do you know?—had in fact never arrived, and so he had to play on a tinny backstage practice piano for a performance that would become one of his most famous recordings, ever. But how many times had Caldon himself been told to just make do, to wing it, that it wasn't about the materials you were given but what you did with them? The lesser piano prevailed, after all, Caldon thought, as Jeb, the neighbor's dog, trailed after him, because Jarrett himself prevailed. Plain and simple. He dug out a fistful of quarters when he reached the pay phone and dialed up Willow.

"I don't understand," he said, absentmindedly petting Jeb's head. Jeb wagged his tail. What did he care that some German thinker died?

"Why would anyone send me a photo of a dead man? This dead man? What do I care if Helmut Krämer is dead?" Caldon said it, for the sake of stating it out loud to his sister, but now that his words hovered in the air, they sounded petty, idiotic, even to him. He did care, but didn't like that he cared. He'd have been perfectly fine if he never knew Helmut had died.

Willow still lived above the cheese shop, in their childhood home just off Mott Street. She'd seen the obituary in the paper. Of course she did. So did the rest of the city.

"I saved it for you. He was pretty famous," she said. "A thinker. Wrote several books about India. And grief." The same black-bordered envelope had also been sent to her, but addressed to Caldon, along with an invitation to the memorial from the Goethe Society.

"It's all in German," Caldon said, pinching one of Jeb's fleas from his wrist. "Why send it to me? We went to school together. Weren't really friends. I hardly liked the guy." He held up the funeral photo of Helmut again. Damn. He really was still handsome, broken nose and all. "You went on a few dates with him, right?" Caldon asked. "Way back?"

"Who didn't? All the girls did," Willow said. "He was quite the catch back then, if you know what I mean. Ah, Helmut, gone too soon! Hey, it looks like that memorial for him? By Goethe? Is tonight. At Essenszeit. You should come."

Caldon didn't want to come, but wouldn't say no. Willow knew this about him and pressed him. He was in Vermont, after all. It was late summer. And he wanted, needed, to be pressed to leave the cool rural wilds for the steamy city.

"I can't imagine what you do out there, hiding out all day in that cabin," she said. "Come home. We won't even tell Mary."

Caldon held his breath, contemplating. If he could get back and air out his suit, and got in the car in an hour, if he could get the car to start in the first place, he'd... just then, the Trailways bus pulled into the station, breaking the silence. The doors opened and there emerged a few well-dressed children with backpacks along with some grandmother-types. Willow got animated as she heard all the way from TriBeCa the rattle of the diesel engine. Caldon inhaled deep the fumes from the city and put another few quarters into the phone.

"That's the city bus, isn't it?" Willow said. "Just get on it and I'll pick you up at Grand Central this afternoon."

"Shoes," he said. "I'm not..."

"The gas station should have flip flops or something if you're barefoot. Lord knows they've got everything else under the sun. Besides, we'll find you something. I've got some of dad's old clothes."

Jeb looked up at him, clearly concerned, but Caldon gestured up the road and said, "go home, Jeb!" in a low tone. And he did. When the bus pulled out ten minutes later, Caldon was on it, sporting a hot pink pair of men's-sized flip flops, holding a *New York Times*, and unwrapping a plastic-wrapped sleeve of powdered donuts across the aisle from a small child. The donut powder got everywhere: on his overalls, on the seat, on the photograph. His hands were matted with the dense white sugar and he sucked on each finger and wiped them on the pant cuff of his overalls as the child watched, insane with donut hunger.

"You know any German?" Caldon asked the child. The child, a girl of about six, stared at the donut. He had held it like he would a dog treat for Jeb. She nodded, cake-dazed.

"If you can read this, I'll give you the last donut."

The child took the photograph into her hands. The oil from his fingers left visible imprints on the photo.

"It's a sleeping man."

"What else?"

"He wants to show you what he looks like when he's tired. He is dreaming, surrounded by flowers, and he has a little girl with big hands who picks the flowers and lays one on his shirt so when he wakes up, he'll see the flower and think of her."

She handed back the photo and held out her hand for the donut.

"You think he has a daughter, then?" he said, looking at the photo. He bit absent-mindedly into the donut.

"Sure he does," she said.

"You don't know German, do you?" he said. He offered the bitten donut to her anyway. She shook her head, angry, refusing his germs. He set it on the armrest, in case she changed her mind, and when the bus stopped in traffic on the Tappan Zee Bridge, the donut lurched forward and landed under the seat in front of them. Instead of reading the paper, he looked out the window and thought about a daughter. His daughter, Josie, handing out flowers at age six, a boy in a dress, all the way down the Palisades and into the city. We didn't take a picture of her in her coffin, he thought.

"*GUTEN TAG!*" said a bottle-blonde lady in lederhosen.

"We're here for the Krämer memorial?" said Willow, looking with horror at the bar's tacky Oktoberfest decor. Essenszeit. Caldon hung back. He hadn't been in a bar—a real bar, Donovan's in Vermont didn't count—in years. In a wall of mirrors, he caught glimpses of himself, the puffy-white storm cloud of hair, like a fuzzed-out Q-tip, hair like he'd always wanted when he was a kid, a few days' worth of whiskers, and his farmer's overalls, speckled with donut dust. A first-class hick. The memorial would have to take him as-is, donut dust and pink flip-flops and all. They got stuck in traffic and rolled in just around 6:30, and as he made his way from the underbelly of the station, realized he forgot Helmut's photo, along with *The Times*, on the Greyhound. Willow met him at Grand Central and instead of stopping home, she handed him one of their father's old tweed sportscoats—"I couldn't find any shoes," she'd said—and they hauled off directly in a cab to Essenszeit.

Just behind the biergarten, where a man on stage actually played an oompah tune on an accordion, was a quieter function room for Helmut's memorial. Of course, the Goethe Society would run the same funeral photograph of Helmut, blown up larger than life, behind a small lectern under one of Helmut's more popular tenets: "*Intelligenz durch Trauer.*" Intelligence through grief, it stated in English underneath, in parentheses, almost as an afterthought. Another: "*Verbindung durch angst.*" Connection through fear. Someone from the Goethe Society was handing out bilingual pamphlets of Helmut's key papers.

"What are these stupid slogans?" Caldon muttered to Willow, as someone handed him a bright green trifold sheet with "Verbindung" plastered across the top. "Some kind of party favor?"

"Shhhh, everyone will hear you," she said. "It's his philosophies."

"How is our grief going to bring us intelligence? Huh. Hey, you know that joke? If you have to tell someone you love them, say it really loud… in German?"

"Really, Caldon?"

"So it will confuse…"

"Enough!"

"and terrify them! It's true! *Danke schein…*"

Willow, in her perfect New York mourning pantsuit, slung her purse over her shoulder and waded through the throngs of people to find seats. She fit right in with the rest of the nattily dressed crowd of thinkers and hangers-on, probably every philosopher and Germanophile, who'd apparently read and translated all of his works ("*Verbindung durch angst*"), every grad student he'd ever mentored, all of Helmut's neighbors from his renovated brownstone Brooklyn co-op, generations of grown émigré cousins and their spawn, a few still-there ancient great aunts who'd raised him, and in the front row, sobbing, in a black linen dress and massive hat to match, was Mary.

It had been a while. Two years, at least. Mary in the front row. He wasn't expecting her. Or the hat.

Mary hadn't seen them yet, but it was only a matter of time.

"I'm gonna find a seat further back," Caldon said. "If I need an escape hatch. Or a *bier*. From the *garten*."

"Okay, you lead," Willow said. Caldon picked his way back through the crowd, trying not to notice the wide berth people gave him, as though he smelled bad, or perhaps on account of his clothes, which were not hipster retro shabby chic fake farmer at a funeral, but rather simply *rural* in a space that was decidedly *urban*, to say nothing of his pink flip-flops and the off-season sports coat. Of course, the first time in two years that Mary would see him, he'd look like a failed Vermont farmer. When they finally found seats, a set of headphones, courtesy of the Goethe Society—each ear cup stated so in all caps—lay at his feet.

"For the translation," Willow said, setting her headphones on her own Q-tip white curls, the feminine, upper-class iteration of Caldon's. The memorial started, in German (of course), with Igor Levit himself flown in special from Berlin to play the *Moonlight Sonata*. A flash of cameras fluttered under the dais where Levit played. What's the press doing here? Caldon thought, as another round of flashes burst like dull dud fireworks. Didn't he already get his own free news obit in *The Times*? He knew personally how expensive a paid obituary cost, even though the details of Josie's death were in all the papers the summer she died. He balked at paying for the obit—$50 a line, with about 28 letters (letters! not even words!) per line—as Mary tended to write long, and in the end her beautiful $6,000 tribute to their only child was never published, not in *The Times*, at least. And while Josie's funeral was private, a steady stream of her childhood friends and college pals emerged for the wake, and they, the grieving parents, had to stand before their own child's coffin and witness and console the endless line of tear-streaked youthful faces, their promise and their grief, all of it compounding their own.

As the pianist concluded his moody *Moonlight*, the crowd swept into a profound, unified applause—well deserved, Caldon allowed, a

forceful rendering of Beethoven's finest, the languid notes lingering
with a melancholy of sharper, minor keys, filling the room with
contemplation, and an odd solitude. People around him wept as the
first speaker stood, from the Goethe Society, apparently, but Caldon
didn't bother to listen in to the translated German on his Goethe
headset. Instead, he focused on the back of Mary's large picture hat,
Mary in the front row, slim shoulders hunched. He had an urge to sit
with her, to let her lean into him as his arm curled familiar around her,
to tell her he'd be there for her, even if he hadn't been these past few
years. He'd whisk her back to Vermont and rub her feet and show her
how he'd fixed up the place. Retiled the bathroom. But really, how had
she known Helmut, beyond the few times they'd socialized at some
event or another, where Helmut was the veritable center of the party?
Ever since he'd become the German thinker, he'd only given Caldon,
for all their past times together, a passing nod and a quick "Caldon, my
friend!" thump on the back. Mary, who was a magazine editor, always
dragged Caldon from one semi-swanky pseudo-intellectual affair to
the next, seeking out story angles, sources, the occasional advertising
prospect. She knew how to work the crowd and Caldon was always
content to let her take the lead. But after Josie died—Josie, lost to them
amid the headlines of yet another transgender woman killed in a hate
crime (it was all over the papers that year, an especially terrible year),
Mary became a shadow of herself. All the awful comments, all the
fears that Caldon had shared with Mary—never to Josie, he simply
couldn't to Josie directly—about their son's decision to become a
daughter, a woman, collapsed onto itself and ruined them. Ruined
their marriage. Mary threw it all back at him, blamed him for his
inability to accept Josie for who she was, for naming aloud the worry
that she'd be killed. And nothing he could say or do would convince
her that those early days of adjustment—the memories re-imprinted,
from stating "son" to "daughter" to "child" in casual reference—were
over. Caldon had loved Josie for who she was, and he grew into a better
person, a more open person, because of her. After the funeral, he
figured Mary needed some space, from him, from the vibrant career
she'd been building, from the city that took from them their only child,

and with as little fanfare as possible, he put in for retirement from the library, pulled the ancient Subaru out of long-term parking, and drove up to Vermont. Because what had he learned, really, from all of this loss? That grief brings intelligence? Willow always told him he might actually benefit from some time away, to account for his role in all that had unfolded—but it wasn't his fault that his son became a daughter, and that some fucko bigot targeted her and killed her behind Webster Hall. Or was it?

But now here was Mary standing—what was Mary doing, approaching the podium? What would she even say about Helmut? The black hat shrouded her pale face, and her eyes, while bright and icy-blue, were wet with pain. And as she launched in, offering a throaty, tearful start to her testament, the projector cast the *"Intelligenz durch Trauer"* slogan across her body, her silver page boy bob, her black picture hat.

"Helmut and I had known each other for years, but it wasn't until after the death of my daughter that we became close…" Caldon inhaled deeply, and understood. Willow glanced toward him, absorbing his shock by reaching out, clasping her hand over his, like a seatbelt strapping him in. How had she moved on? Whatever it was that had happened, weren't they still—married? Something? Wasn't he showing her respect by giving her space, and yet here she was grieving over this German thinker like his mourning lover. Or, not *like* his mourning lover, but *as* his mourning lover. His urge to stand overwhelmed him, to speak out to Mary as though they were the only two in the room, but Willow kept her grip on his hand, reinforcing firmly, into his thigh, commanding him further into his seat, now hard and plastic, all angles. The photo of Helmut in his coffin, in Køln, loomed above Mary as she told the story. Apparently, she'd joined him on a brief lecture circuit throughout much of Bavaria and into Wiesbaden, then, Stuttgart, before they drove up to Køln so she could meet his mother — "a lovely woman," Mary reported to the audience, "strong, even in her 90s; she'd be thrilled to know how much he meant to New York"—and then Mary had returned to the States, leaving Helmut with his mother in Køln to sort out some family business.

"And then the heart attack. I always thought I'd see him again," she said, "He was one of the most brilliant men I'd ever known."

Oh, brilliant, Caldon thought. Why no mention that she was still married, and where did her old husband, the one who she spent twenty-six years of her life with, who was the brilliant father of the brilliant child who'd also died, calculate into Helmut's brilliance? Hadn't he, after all, been the one to introduce them? And how long, exactly, had she waited to bask in his brilliance after Caldon had moved to Vermont? The menagerie of questions kept swirling, rendered by humiliation, then ire, then jealousy, then grief, all of it revived anew, for Josie, for their marriage, for his stupid pink flip flops he thought he'd get away with wearing. And now here he was, the slob of a not-quite-ex-husband in overalls and his dead father's mothball coat, showing up to hear how the German thinker—and lover—was, in all imaginable ways, from their days on the tennis court to romancing his wife to comforting her after Josie died, to being honored at his memorial by one of the world's foremost pianists, the better man in his tiny shitbox of a life.

As though Willow understood the river of his mind, where the rocks and rapids of his memory would undoubtedly take him, she clamped down even further on his hand, pinning his thigh into the chair with her gym-toned biceps. And as Mary sat down, and as Igor Levit resumed his spot at the bench to play one more sonata. "*Pathetique*," he joked, "an unfitting title, because Helmut was anything but," yet it was one of his favorites. "Let us find, together, as Helmut did, the levity in the absurd," Igor Levit said, "as we honor the passing of our dear friend."

Caldon felt Willow's grip on him relax, and he took that moment, as Igor Levit launched into the first few bars of the piece—a crashing lively spray of notes that normally he'd relish getting lost in, hearing each plunk and shine of the piano overlap and trip through the air— he stood, finally, slipping out of Willow's grasp, and headed, not out toward the *biergarten*, toward the tacky oompah crowd and the lederhosen ladies, for a much needed stein and a jag of currywurst, but rather toward the pianist, the podium, toward Mary. Mary. He called out to her as the melody of the song unfolded, and she turned and saw him, her eyebrows arched in surprise, just as the thong of the pink flip flop loosened itself and he tripped, tumbling, as the air in his chest tightened, then surged up to his throat, closing off oxygen, freezing his muscles, his heart, before he collapsed on the ground. As the murmur of concern moved through the audience, and as the well of news photographers descended upon him, the last thing he saw, as the pianist played on, was not the popping flash of cameras or the face of first Willow, and then Mary, standing over him, their faces etched with concern, or guilt, respectively, nor the large funeral photo of Helmut Krämer, or the lingering notes of *"Pathetique,"* but rather that of Josie, back when he was Joseph, in the earliest part of summer in Vermont, little Joseph in one of Willow's old smocked dresses he'd discovered in a closet. Joseph, standing before the bramble, in the bright of the day, who'd just eaten a blackberry green, his mouth puckered with sour and delight, holding out another in his outstretched palm, asking, "When's it gonna change, Poppa? When?"

WITH GRATITUDE

A SPECIAL THANKS to my beloved first reader and editor Luke Whisnant; to my parents, Robert and Linda Plouffe, and other members of my family (especially Jilly, Avery, and Colby), who have always inspired and cheered on my creative endeavors; to my small band of artists and writers who've offered insight and thoughtful conversation about art and letters and music everything in between: Sarah Anderson, Mercy Carbonell, Carla Collins, Allison Devers, Ellee Dean, Nicole Dunas, David Gates (and the rest of the Dog House Band), Elaine Fletcher Chapman, Elena Gosalvez-Blanco, Val Haynes, Tim Horvath, Kathy Hughes, Lee Clay Johnson, David Joseph, Devi Lockwood, Yvonne Mazurek, Cat Parnell, Nancy McGillicuddy Rapavi, Denise Rodgers, and Kim Young; to my colleagues at Phillips Exeter Academy and the George W. Bennett Fellowship, and their continued support of my projects and adventures; to all of my teachers at Bennington College, East Carolina University, the University of Massachusetts at Amherst, and Southbridge High School (particularly the late Sally Byrne); to all of my students, who never stop inspiring me; and to the writing communities I have found at the Vermont Studio Center, Bread Loaf, the Community of Writers in Olympic Valley, the Summer Literary Seminars, the Wildacres Retreat, Bennington College, and East Carolina University; to the North Carolina Arts Council; to contest judge Nick White; and finally, to David Bowen, Scott Mashlan, Brian Herrick, Brian Matzat, and Angelo Maneage at New American Press and Julia Borcherts and Jordan Brown at Kaye Publicity for their interest in and care for my work.

ERICA PLOUFFE LAZURE is the author of three chapbooks, *Sugar Mountain* (Ad Hoc Press, 2020), *Heard Around Town* (Arcadia, 2015), and *Dry Dock* (Arcadia, 2015). She is a former newspaper reporter who now writes, teaches English, and draws in Exeter, New Hampshire. She can be found online at www.ericaplouffelazure.com.